THE GRAY LOVER

THREE STORIES

ALSO BY CARL FRIEDMAN

Nightfather (1994)

The Shovel and the Loom (1996)

THE GRAY LOVER

THREE STORIES

CARL FRIEDMAN

Translated from the Dutch by Jeannette K. Ringold

A Karen and Michael Braziller Book

PERSEA BOOKS

New York

Originally published under the title *De grauwe minnaar* in 1996
by Uitgeverij G. A. van Oorschot, Amsterdam.
First published in the United States of America in 1998 by Persea Books, New York.

For information, write to the publisher:
Persea Books, Inc.
171 Madison Avenue
New York, New York 10016

Library of Congress Cataloging-in-Publication Data

Friedman, Carl
[Grauwe minnaar. English]
The gray lover : three stories / by Carl Friedman : translated
from the Dutch by Jeannette K. Ringold.
p. cm.
Contents: The gray lover—Holy fire—Bette.
ISBN 0-89255-232-8 (hard. : alk. paper)
1. Jews—Fiction. I. Title.
PT5881. 16.R48G713 1998   97-24007
839.3'1364—dc21   CIP

Designed by Rita Lascaro

FIRST EDITION

CONTENTS

The Gray Lover
1

Holy Fire
39

Bette
105

THE GRAY LOVER

And he was driven from the sons of men,
and his heart was made like the beasts,
and his dwelling was with the wild asses.
                                    —Daniel 5:21

W HEN HANNA KATZ WAS ALMOST ONE HUNDRED years old, she'd had enough of this world. She washed herself, put on her shawl that she had kept in the linen closet, and stretched out on her bed. While singing "Adon Olam" (*Into His hands I entrust my spirit, when I go to sleep*), she closed her eyes. This happened about midday. The sun, shining through the window, tried to change her mind by tickling her thin gray eyelashes, but Hanna didn't let herself be persuaded. Whoever doesn't know after one hundred years what he wants was born for naught. Hanna knew what she wanted. She died, and that was that. When the women of the small funeral society of Slomniki arrived, they found her lying there ready, as if she expected the Messiah to come at any moment, and it seemed hardly worth the trouble to bury her body, that body that would arise and dance at His coming.

Her husband, Gershom, was so many years past one hundred that the exact number eluded him and didn't matter anymore. During his long existence he had survived small and large pogroms, two Polish uprisings, and one world war. He had worked as miller's servant and as saddlemaker, as tinker and as porter. He knew that the ways of men are even more inscrutable than the ways of God, but he had never complained about it, no more than a dog complains about his tail. Every morning he had said his prayers in the village synagogue. Every evening he had drunk too much brandy and had told tall tales in the village tavern. In short, he had paid attention to the words of Ecclesiastes: "Do not live too righteously or too wisely. Why should you cause yourself vexation?"

After Hanna had departed in her own stubborn way, Gershom had to manage for himself, all alone in the house at the edge of the village. Step by step he shuffled across the yard, his stick creaking under the weight of his back, which bent forward at a right angle. He did nothing remarkable. He mumbled something to a lizard warming itself in the heat of summer. He smiled at a couple of chickens fighting over a potato peel. He looked at the blue sky and listened to the chirping of crickets with the absorption of a man who never has to rush again.

Gershom had no cares. When one Jew itches, twenty immediately come forward to scratch. The village women took turns baking bread for him. Yankel the butcher put meat aside. And Schloime the peddler sometimes provided him with a pound of sugar, other times with a piece of soap or a new wick for his oil lamp. Everything was in perfect order.

But at the end of the month of Tishri, a few days after the Rejoicing of the Law, the region was hit by an early winter. In one single night a storm blew all the leaves off the trees. The following day the windows were thickly frosted. From the gutters in which sparrows had made their nests just a short while ago, icicles the size of tusks glistened. Then it began to snow in small, sharp flakes, which stung the skin of men and animals. Soon the church tower, the houses, and the spruces on the hills around Slomniki were wearing white miters. Gershom was cold. Neighbors came by to cut wood and to light his stove, but he let the fire die down as soon as they were gone. Nor was the fire the only thing that he forgot. Even the chickens were neglected. In the snow-covered shed they dropped dead, falling off their roost, one after the other. In the end, Gershom neglected himself as well. Night after night he lay down to sleep in the clothes he had been wearing when he got up in the morning, and finally he no longer made the effort to get out of bed. When one of the village women found the bread left by her predecessor untouched and Gershom motionless, she became alarmed.

Rabbi Yehuda Zipkin was called in. He was the right person for this matter, because he combined the insight of a man of study and prayer with the thoroughness of a farmer. In his snow-covered overcoat he walked straight to the bed in which the bent shape of Gershom was outlined under rags and a moth-eaten sheepskin. With one movement of his hand, the rabbi exposed him to daylight, but Gershom continued to lie still, like a child who pretends to be asleep.

"This can't go on any longer!" said the rebbe. "You stink like a pot of spoiled bean soup. Do you want to be like Job, who became covered with worms while he was still alive?"

"Did Job stink like spoiled bean soup?" whispered Gershom. "This is the first time I've heard that." He opened his eyes. They were filled with tears, the only liquid that hadn't turned to ice in the prevailing temperature.

Rabbi Yehuda sighed. Other elderly people moved in with their children, even before they required looking after. But the two sons that Hanna had borne had died at birth. Gershom no longer had any family. His last relative, a cousin on his father's side, had been arrested by the Russian authorities during the uprising of 1863 and had died in prison.

That same afternoon the Jewish villagers gathered in a meeting to discuss the question of Gershom Katz.

"My daughter Miriam can come in the afternoon to sweep the floor, do his laundry, and cook dinner for him," suggested Yankel the butcher.

The rebbe shook his head. "That's not enough. Gershom needs someone who can take care of him day and night. Otherwise he'll come to a bad end. To prevent an accident, your daughter would have to move in with him, but that goes against the law. After all, an unmarried woman and man are not allowed to stay under one roof."

"Gershom a man?" mocked the butcher. "He's as old as Methuselah!"

"Old men are not excluded from the law," said the rebbe. "And that's all to the good. Methuselah was one hundred eighty-seven years old when he begot Lemech."

"And Lemech begot Noah. And Noah was five hundred years old when he begot Shem," the butcher said with a wink. "I wonder how they managed that at their age. They no longer had a tooth in their mouths!"

At this, Golek the baker jumped up. He found it necessary to remind the butcher that man does not reproduce with his teeth.

"Fortunately not," answered Yankel, "for if that were the case, the Jews of Slomniki would have died out long ago. Everyone breaks his jaws on that so-called fresh bread of yours!"

Those present laughed, but when the discussion threatened to become too lively, Rabbi Yehuda slammed both his hands on the table. In the silence that followed, Sam Petscher stepped forward. To everyone's surprise, he declared that he

CARL FRIEDMAN

was ready to take old Gershom into his home. But, he added, he wouldn't do it for nothing. Gershom would have to sell his possessions at auction and hand the money over to him in exchange for room and board.

Much bad was said about Sam Petscher, and not one word was a lie. Certainly he had such an ugly face that he was considered one of their own by the Polish farmers from the area. Certainly he was a nitwit. He brimmed with so much stupidity that his eyes bulged. Certainly he was miserly. No beggar ate at his table on the Sabbath. And he most certainly cursed like a Cossack. He never came to the house of prayer, not even on Yom Kippur, when even confirmed sinners are brought to repent by the sound of the ram's horn.

Sam lived in a house with a sagging roof and cracked walls. It consisted of one room that he shared against his will with a skinny cow, a goat, some chickens, and with his wife Ruchel, whom he considered to be of the same order as cattle. While all the creatures around him made themselves useful, Sam himself didn't lift a finger. The chickens laid eggs, the cow gave milk, and Ruchel wove baskets from willows. Even the piece of property that they owned was more productive than he, for it produced onions, beets, and other crops. The only thing that Sam cultivated was the flesh on his backside, and that grew without any effort on his part.

He bestirred himself only once a week, on Thursdays. Then he let himself be awakened by Ruchel at the crack of dawn. In the dark he'd eat a bowlful of lukewarm barley groats. After that, he'd kick the goat outdoors and hitch it to a cart, which Ruchel had loaded with milk, eggs, vegetables, and baskets. Grumbling, Sam trudged beside the goat to the local market. His mood didn't improve until he had sold his wares and could start hitting the bottle in the tavern. After midnight he'd head home. But then, like an enormous sack of flour, he sat on the cart himself, for why should you make life easy for a goat that lives at your expense? Bleating plaintively, the animal staggered down the village street with its heavy load, while the wheels of the cart squeaked and Sam jabbered away. Many a villager, jolted awake by the racket, would sigh: "There they go again. The goat is pulling the pig."

Sam Petscher cared only for Sam Petscher. About others he couldn't care less. But no sooner had he heard in the tavern that the rabbi was looking for people to watch over Gershom Katz than a plan began to brew in his head.

"We're getting a boarder," he said to Ruchel when he woke from his hangover the next day.

She was furiously stirring a pot of steaming beet soup. "What do you mean, a boarder?" she asked suspiciously as she wiped the spatters from her cheek with her sleeve.

"Just like I'm telling you," Sam said, yawning. He showed no signs of getting out of bed. "A boarder, someone who's going to eat and sleep here."

"For that we need to take on a boarder?" Ruchel said sarcastically. "I think that more than enough eating and drinking is being done by you. You don't mean to tell me that you need help with it?" She threw the lid on the pan and placed her hands on her hips. "The gentleman is too pathetic to kill his own lice. The gentleman lies in bed all day and lets himself be fed and watered. He puts on the airs of a prince." Her face glistening with sweat, she made a curtsy: "His Highness Prince Radziwill Fatass, at your service! If I didn't pull off his boots every evening, they would grow onto his feet. The roof is falling apart over his head. Over here the chickens are flapping about, and over there the cow is mooing. But the gentleman wants to take in a boarder. God knows where I can get the money to fatten another idler like you!"

Unmoved, Sam cleared his throat, sat up halfway, and spat on the floor. Then he let himself flop back again with a thud. "It isn't just any boarder," he said, "it's bent-over Gershom. He doesn't eat much, and he's as good as dead. And because charity is hard work, we're letting him pay for it—that goes without saying."

"What good will it do me?" shouted Ruchel. "The only one who'll get rich off our money is the tavern keeper!" Angrily, she approached him. "Who milks the cow around here? It's me. Who keeps the stove burning and the house clean? Who cuts the willows and weaves baskets? Who works in the field? It's me. And who lives it up from those earnings? It's the gentleman, because the gentleman drinks like a sponge. At night, when he comes home dead drunk, I have to look through his pockets in the dark, like a thief. And then I can thank heaven when I find a handful of groshen!"

"It's the goat's fault," said Sam, aggrieved. "You'd also get a dry throat if you had to trudge to the village with that broken-down animal. That goat has had his day. He can't keep going. All the peddlers in the market sneer at him."

"At you or at the goat?" scoffed Ruchel.

But Sam wrapped his arms around her thighs so that she lost her balance and fell over him onto the bed. "Oh, Ruchele, Ruchele, you're so hard-hearted," he said. "And just when I was planning to mend my ways and to buy a donkey." He pushed his lips into her skinny neck.

Ruchel, who hadn't been touched by him in years, unless it was to get a beating, was flattered and giggled. "Why a donkey?"

"Because a donkey can pull more than a goat. With a donkey before the cart I'll get to the village much faster."

"Without being bothered by a dry throat?"

He nodded. "If I had a donkey, you'd never have to search through my pockets again. There would be enough money, because I'd take my wares to Miechowki and Proszowice, to the farthest markets around. Of course a horse is more beautiful but also more expensive to own. A donkey needs very little care. He eats kitchen scraps and thistles. With a leather harness in front and a sturdy whip on his behind, a donkey becomes a horse."

On impulse he pushed up Ruchel's skirt, but at the sight of her pale, bony legs, he turned his back on her.

A little later he was snoring again.

As soon as Gershom moved in with the Petschers, Sam went looking for a donkey to buy. Toward evening, he came home, too numbed with cold to curse, on the back of the animal. It was a young, slate-gray male. He had clearly been well cared for by his former owner. Everything on him was shiny, even his bridle and bit. He showed no sign of the apathy with which many of his sort, dulled by years of mistreatment, resign themselves to their lot. He wasn't the kind of donkey to be reconciled to just any kind of lot. On the contrary, even in the somber house of the Petschers, he swished his tail energetically. In his eyes shone the temperament of his wild Nubian forefathers. He also brayed frequently. With his head up and his ears drawn back, he bared his teeth. Then he snorted, squeaking like a pair of old bellows, and next he exhaled with a penetrating throaty sound that seemed to tear his vocal cords. But this never happened, for after each sound there followed another that was even more off-key and more triumphant.

The other animals were invigorated by this. The chickens laid eggs with more dedication. The cow gave two full buckets of milk daily. And the old goat attempted a small skip whenever the donkey brayed. But no amount of jumping could save the goat now. He was taken to the butcher and returned as meat for roasting.

From the goatskin, Ruchel cut a pair of leggings for Sam. As promised, he traveled to markets in the area, with the donkey pulling the cart. But he didn't keep this up for more than a few weeks. When the newness was gone, he again lay in bed every day except Thursday. There, with a bottle of slivovitz within reach, he did his best to convince Ruchel that their boarder urgently needed to be put to work.

She was doubtful.

"Have you ever looked at him carefully?" she whispered, pointing at Gershom. "His hands tremble like the fish pudding my mother, blessed be her memory, used to make, and all his bones creak. Besides, he's no longer right in the head."

Sam waved away all her objections. "It's simply a question of not enough exercise," he said breezily. "All that sitting still makes him stiff and sluggish. We've got to give him something to do: milk the cow, brush the donkey, get water. That's our duty to him."

Ruchel hesitated. "Are you sure? He can barely walk, he's as bent as a hairpin."

"That's the problem," contended Sam. "He keeps growing more bent over. How can he ever be buried? He won't fit in any coffin! If we leave him to his lot, he'll miss out on eternity."

"Do you think that we'll be able to straighten him?"

"No," said Sam, "he'll never be as straight as an arrow—

that's pushing it. But we can bend him back quite a bit. Healthy exercise does wonders." He grinned so that his rotted teeth became visible. "You don't begrudge him a proper funeral, or do you?"

Ruchel squeezed her eyes to slits. "Of course not," she said, hesitating. And then, from the bottom of her heart: "The sooner the better!"

The Petschers were serious about their duty to their fellow man. They gave Gershom so much exercise that it became a day's work for him. In the dark of the morning, like a factory whistle, the cow mooed him awake. Dizzy with sleep, he crawled to the foot of his straw mattress where, with stiff fingers, he put on his clothes and his shoes. While the cow mooed relentlessly, he lit the lamp. From the kettle on the cold stove, he scooped water to wash his hands and face. Then he started the morning prayer: *I thank You, living and constant God; You returned my soul to me when I awakened.*

In the bed on the other side of the room there was a commotion. Sam began to yell in order to make himself heard over the cow's racket and Gershom's singing. "When are you planning to push a bucket under that animal?" he screamed, threatening. "If you keep on harping about your soul, that cow will give vinegar instead of milk!" Cursing, he fell back to sleep.

Gershom sat down next to the cow and began pulling her teats mechanically. While the milk filled the bucket in rhythmic jets, he thought about things. He didn't know how and why he had landed in this strange house, but he understood that his host and hostess meant him no good. They made him carry wood for the stove and clear out manure. He even had to scrub the stone floor on his knees with a strong soap. They drove him from morning till night, and he didn't dare protest. He was at the mercy of their whims. Although God especially loves the weak, He helps the strong.

Sometimes Gershom used his nails to scratch some ice from the window so that he could look outside. White as a shroud, snow covered the fields. He envied Hanna, who lay carefree in the earth waiting for the time when the Messiah would come and the mountains would flow with sweet wine.

The donkey's life was even more difficult. Because the animal barely reacted to the whip, Sam had bought an iron rod with a pointed end, the kind used by donkey drivers to prod recalcitrant animals. In Sam's grip this instrument became a deadly weapon, one that he wielded alternately as a spear or a club.

Initially, he beat the donkey only on Thursdays and always for a good reason. He complained to Ruchel about the stubbornness of the animal, which refused to budge on the way to the village. "It's always the same story. You can't even see the church tower yet, when there he goes; that piece of misery takes his time eating from the feedbag!" he said to justify the bloody stripes on the donkey's back.

But there is nothing human hands get used to more easily

than to whipping. After some time Sam's hands no longer needed any excuse for beating. The least provocation sufficed. Sometimes the animal would be beaten because he stamped his hooves too eagerly, and other times because he looked too lethargic for Sam's liking. Sometimes he ate too greedily and other times not greedily enough. Even the slightest wrong movement by the animal could cause Sam to burst out in blind anger.

As soon as he'd pull out the iron rod, the donkey would start braying indignantly. "There, now you see it yourself!" he shouted over his shoulder to Ruchel. "That mangy animal is mocking me to my face. But he'll get over that fast, I promise you!"

There are people who bite their nails or pick their noses out of boredom. When Sam Petscher couldn't think of anything to do, he'd attack his donkey.

In the month of Shevat, after the Polish farmers had celebrated Christmas and New Year's Day with much bell ringing, the snow continued to fall. In an uninterrupted offensive, stinging flakes hurled themselves against the village, which became isolated from the world. The Jews of Slomniki didn't understand where all that snow had come from.

When they asked Rabbi Yehuda, he shrugged his shoulders. "Even the Almighty is sometimes guilty of exaggeration," he said. "Consider yourselves lucky that He chose snow. It could have been worse; just think of Sodom and Gomorrah."

This image didn't frighten them off. On the contrary, many had practically gone through their fuel supply and would have liked to see some fire and brimstone come down from Heaven.

After a while, people became silent and withdrawn, as though it snowed not only outside but indoors as well, between husband and wife, between mother and child. Gershom Katz seemed to have been forgotten by everyone. He had even disappeared from the thoughts of the rabbi. Every trace of the old man seemed to have been erased by the snow.

The Jewish community of Slomniki was not very prosperous and not very large. In total it consisted of a few hundred souls. Most of them lived in the streets around the market square, because that's where the house of prayer and the house of learning were located. In ugly small stores, which smelled of mildew all year round, the villagers sold their meager wares. One sold fish, another iron. There was a tailor who mostly patched worn pants and caftans. There was a carpenter who knew how to turn two rotted window shutters into one rotted school bench. And there were those who practiced more than one trade, like the bookbinder who also worked as cantor and writer of amulet inscriptions.

The Petschers, on the other hand, lived out of the way. With a few other Jewish families, they lived at the very edge of the village, well past the water mill. Their group of houses was scattered helter-skelter at the bottom of a hill. At a slight distance stood an outhouse for community use. It was a small wooden building with a cesspit underneath and was called the "stinkhouse." Across this pit lay a plank that offered seating for two people but that seldom was occupied by more than one. Whoever left the stinkhouse was always in a hurry—in the summer to escape the flies and in the winter, the cold. Whoever went to it ran even faster, for a visit to the stinkhouse was always postponed not to the last but to the very last moment. Meetings near the latrine had a fleeting character, even when two people in the doorway bumped into each other, each with his pants down to his knees. What they had in common was really an illusion, since the one pair of pants was on its way up and the other on its way down.

It should be added that the stinkhouse was known as the favorite hiding place of evil spirits. Demons and dybbuks of all kinds waited in the cesspit for their chance to enter the bodies of the living, which, under the circumstances, wasn't difficult at all. Everyone in the village knew the story of Motke Fiedler. On a warm afternoon, after a visit to the latrine, he began speaking a formal kind of Polish. To the dismay of his wife and his children, he crossed himself three times before the evening meal. And near bedtime he was in such a bad state that he was singing Latin vespers while standing on his head. His body seemed to have been taken over by the spirit of a medieval bishop from Poznan who had committed so many sins during his lifetime that his soul had not found peace, even almost five hundred years after his death. As soon as this spirit discovered that he had mistakenly landed in a Jew, he escaped as fast as he could through Motke's nose, with the result that since that time Motke has not been able to smell anything, not even horseradish or cinnamon.

Is it true that everyone meets the fate that he deserves, and that the heavenly powers choose for this not only the right time but also the most suitable place?

One morning during Shevat, someone impatiently rattled the Petschers' shutters. Half asleep, first Gershom and then Ruchel headed toward the noise. It was still dark, but the moon threw a blue light on the snow. Outside, their neighbor Faibesh stood panting in his long underwear. His breath steamed. He carried a lantern whose flame flickered restlessly. His beard blew into his face. Distraught, he pointed in the direction of the latrine. "It's Sam!" he stammered.

"What's the matter with Sam?" asked Ruchel, alarmed, pulling her wrap up to her chin.

Faibesh gasped for breath. "He's dead, sitting in the stinkhouse."

Struggling on their spindly legs, Ruchel, Faibesh, and Gershom walked through a high snow bank to the scene of the calamity. In horror, Faibesh had let the door blow out of his hand, and it stood wide open. Inside sat Sam, motionless, his fleshy thighs spread apart and his pants around his ankles. His round head hung sideways, eyes closed and lips swollen purple.

Immediately Ruchel started moaning, calling upon her dead mother as well as the Almighty. In the surrounding houses, lights were turned on. Neighbors came outside, coats and shawls covering their nightclothes. Confusion reigned. Someone threw a sheepskin over the exposed lower part of Sam's body. While a few men spat into the snow to keep the demons away, the women wailed in unison with Ruchel. But their singsong *"Oy veh, oy veh"* stopped abruptly when a boy screamed that he had seen Sam blink his eyes. It became eerily quiet. Faibesh lifted his lantern and took a step forward. With his free hand he carefully shook the dead man's shoulder. Glassy-eyed, Sam glanced at him and groaned. The small crowd flew apart.

"He's still breathing," shouted Faibesh, "he's still breathing!"

And it was true—Sam Petscher was still among the living. In the middle of the night he had returned from the tavern in a delirium and had been overcome by the cold in the stinkhouse. Meanwhile, his behind was frozen stiff to the board.

Here and there people snickered. While Ruchel kept wailing, people ran into their houses to heat water. They poured seven pots and seven kettles over Sam's lap. Only then could he be lifted up and carried away.

The news went through the village like wildfire.

"Have you heard yet?" one Jew said to the next.

"What?"

"Sam Petscher has to stay in bed!"

"Has he ever done anything else in his life?"

Even the farmers in the market made fun of it. A normal person, they shouted to each other from their market stalls, would have frozen to death during such a night on the latrine. But Sam couldn't freeze in twenty years because undiluted alcohol flowed through his veins.

Only the Petschers didn't laugh. Sam could hardly move. His backside had been frozen, and his front had been scalded by the hot water. Groaning, he lay first on one side and then on the other. Twice a day, he turned on to his belly so that Ruchel could place a soothing compress on his behind. She did this deliberately and silently. Since the incident in the stinkhouse she had refused to speak to Sam. Whether he cursed or begged, not a word crossed her thin lips. She couldn't forgive him for bringing shame on her before the eyes of all their neighbors.

The donkey, which had fled during the night of the accident, was found again the next afternoon. Completely crazed, it had trotted across the frozen river. The cart had filled to the top with snow and rumbled behind him. In the evening, two neighbors delivered him to the Petschers. The donkey wouldn't step beyond the door of the hated house, but Gershom finally lured him across the threshold with some lumps of sugar and soothing words.

Three of the four windows had burst from their frames because of the hard frost and had been boarded up, plunging the room into semidarkness. On the table stood an oil lamp that burned during the day, and each sudden draft sent the smell of the smoking wick through the room.

Sam became feverish from the infected wounds. By turns he panted with fever and shivered with chills. When the chickens threw shadows on the walls with their outstretched wings, he covered his face with his hands and mumbled that Asmodai on eagle's wings had come to drag him to Gehenna.

Ruchel, too ashamed to turn to the rebbe, called in the help of cross-eyed Kasha, a Polish witch who was highly regarded by the farmers. Not only did she practice astrology and interpret dreams, but she also cured cattle of the staggers and people of evil spirits.

In the early afternoon she knocked at the Petchers' door. To put the old woman in a good mood, Ruchel gave her a bowl of potato soup, which she slurped down without sitting. Over the edge of the bowl, her right eye leered at the sick person, while the squinting left eye scanned the room.

From one of her purses the crone fished a fistful of sheep bones, which she held in front of Sam's mouth. He gasped for air, but before he could let out a sigh, she turned around three times and opened her fingers. The small bones rolled over the floor like dice. She looked at them and clacked her tongue.

"Is it serious?" asked Ruchel.

The crone didn't answer. She placed her ears next to Sam's skull and listened intently.

"There are no devils in his head," she finally said, "but there are cracks. That's because of the cold. Everything inside has burst."

"Cracks?" said Ruchel, bewildered. "And how can they be closed up?"

Silently Kasha spread a poultice of linseed on the burn wounds and covered Sam's stomach with cabbage leaves. After that she hung the bags around her neck again. She felt in her boot and pulled out a wad of tobacco, which she pushed between her teeth. With slow, bovine stubbornness, she began to chew.

"Well, if he were one of us..." she said, without finishing her sentence.

Ruchel nodded. She knew that Polish farmers could be cured of horrible diseases if, during high mass, they let themselves be carried around the church altar seven times, or if they spent the night of a full moon at the feet of the statue of the Virgin Mother.

"If only you hadn't murdered Jesus Christ," she said, smacking her lips as she wiped the slobber from her chin with the back of her wrinkled hand. "Now you are cursed by Heaven. What can I do about it? Against God's wrath there is no remedy." She wrung the neck of the chicken that Ruchel handed her in payment, threw the still-convulsing animal over her shoulder, and stumbled outdoors, where it was still snowing.

Sam's fever passed and scabs appeared over the wounds, but his head wouldn't heal. Most of the day he lay talking to himself. His moods alternated rapidly. Now he'd shout, roaring with laughter: "No, don't tickle, please don't tickle!" A moment later he'd sing a sentimental song from the time when he had served in the Polish army. *"Dear girl, I've got to go, the drum is sounding, plea-ease save a kiss for your brave soldier."* The rest of the lyrics were lost in sniveling.

Henceforth it was Ruchel who rode to the market on Thursday. She brought home not slivovitz but all sorts of things intended to promote Sam's recovery, from obscure salves and powders to a weather-stained icon, from soothsayers' cards to a wooden statue of Saint Anthony, patron saint of the sick. To that last item she daily mumbled prayers in what Hebrew she remembered from her youth. She hung amulets with Aramaic inscriptions around Sam's neck, and she put a blue wool hat on his head to prevent it from cracking still more. She bought a sack of pebbles from a quack who insisted that he had personally gone to gather them in the Holy Land because they provided protection against the evil eye. Although they couldn't be distinguished from the gravel on the village street, Ruchel placed them in all the corners of the conjugal bed. The pebbles did indeed seem to come from the Holy Land because they, like the Jews, had a talent for wandering. In no time at all they lay scattered all over the mattress, and there they brought about a miracle. Sam, who had been lying down for weeks, sat bolt upright. The glazed look had disappeared from his eyes, which were now flashing with anger. He looked at Ruchel, who was addressing her umpteenth supplication to Saint Anthony.

"Goddamn, am I lying in bed or am I lying on cobblestones?" he roared, exasperated. He grabbed Saint Anthony from the table and tried to crush him with his feet. When this failed, he opened the stove and pushed the statue inside. The dry wood crackled. A fountain of sparks lit up Sam's face. For a moment he seemed bewildered. Slumping, he stared into the flames.

At that very moment the donkey scraped the stone floor with a hoof. Twice a nervous "hee-haw" sounded. Sam flew into a temper. "They're scum," he shouted. "Scum of the earth. When they don't pray, they bray!" He took the donkey's rod from the hearth and stuck it into the fire like a poker, all the while mumbling: "They want to destroy me, they won't rest until I'm completely destroyed."

Ruchel and Gershom held their breath. When Sam finally pulled the rod out of the stove, the tip was red-hot. Swinging the rod, he drove the donkey into a corner. With its full weight, the donkey flung himself against the wall, as through he wanted to disappear into it. When Sam pressed the hot iron into his flank and the stench of singed hair spread through the room, the donkey cringed even more.

With small, shaky steps Gershom ran up to throw himself between Sam and the donkey, but his bent back threw him off-balance. He landed on the floor next to the donkey, where Sam immediately started kicking him. "Filthy animal!" he shouted. "Butcher's dog!" With his rod, he burned one of the elbows with which Gershom was protecting his head. Didn't Sam hear Ruchel scream? In his confusion did Sam no longer see the difference between the old man and the donkey? Sweat streamed from under his hat and his amulets rattled wildly as he brought the iron down on the donkey's backside and then again on Gershom's shoulders.

Then, as suddenly as his fury had come over him, Sam became calm. His fists relaxed, and his chin sank to his chest. He hummed one of his soldier's songs. Not until he had remained still for a while did Ruchel dare to lead him back to bed. As soon as he was asleep, she threw the rod into the snow behind the house.

Lying on his straw mattress, Gershom started to shake. Where could Hanna be? She hadn't come for a very long time. Had she lost her way and been overtaken by darkness? With a pounding heart, he peered into the dark. Were those Hanna's footsteps that he heard, or those of the man with the amulets?

But neither Hanna nor the man with the amulets showed up. The only thing that came toward him out of the night was the head of the donkey. He moved his large tongue slowly over Gershom's face, as though licking salt from a stone. Then Gershom decided to give the animal a name. He called it Menachem: he who consoles.

In the month of Adar, it began to thaw. And the month of Nisan brought wind from the southwest, which blew the mud from the paths. When the swallows returned to move into their old nests under the eaves, Gershom was sent to the field. Every morning he climbed to the other side of the hill with Menachem, who carried spade, hoe, and seeds for sowing. The trip was difficult, but that didn't matter. A burden fell from Gershom's shoulders as soon as he left the stuffy house in which Sam mumbled to the walls and Ruchel to her icon.

Now that the village had awakened from its hibernation, the secret that Gershom Katz was working himself to the bone on the property of the Petschers was out.

"Can you believe it? Stooped Gershom is now digging in Sam's field."

"It can't be true. That's no way to make someone spend his last days!"

"I swear to you, every day he's sent up the hill like any pimple-faced farm hand!"

What was the world coming to, the Jews of Slomniki said to one another, when defenseless old people were being used as doormats? For the sake of convenience, they blamed the rabbi. Wasn't he the one who had personally agreed to let poor, stooped Gershom move in with Sam, who had a screw loose, and Ruchel, who consorted with quacks and witches?

When Rabbi Yehuda Zipkin heard of their reproaches, he groaned with regret. Quickly he put on his hat. With resolute steps he walked briskly to the water mill and up the hill. A little later he stood facing Gershom who, leaning on his spade, lifted his foot to show him a hole in the sole of his shoe. The old man seemed to think that he was the village cobbler.

Panting, the rabbi said: "Don't you recognize me? I'm the rebbe."

"But you look exactly like the cobbler."

"Still, I'm not the cobbler. What would a cobbler be doing here?"

"Who did you say you were?"

"The rebbe," repeated Rabbi Yehuda. Wringing his hands, he burst out in a confession of guilt. "But I didn't know it. You must believe me. All that time I didn't know, it's a misunderstanding."

Gershom nodded. "So you too thought that you were a cobbler. You don't have to be ashamed of that; it's happened to me. I don't know whether I'm dreaming or awake. I'm no longer surprised at anything." He sighed. "But if it's true that you're the rebbe, then you've come at the right moment. Hanna and I are planning to marry. We want to set a date for the wedding."

Rabbi Yehuda's eyes filled with tears when he realized that

Gershom had become senile. Apologies no longer made sense. The old man was living in the present as well as in a gray past. Everything in between was cloudy. His youth was clearer in his memory than was yesterday.

"Come," the rebbe said hoarsely, "you have to get away from here, you're coming home with me. You won't find the fleshpots of Egypt, but where seven are eating, an eighth can join as well."

"And a ninth?" Gershom pointed to the donkey that was grazing in the adjoining meadow.

"That donkey belongs to Sam Petscher," said the rebbe. "I know that he bought it with money that was yours. But you can't take the animal with you—that would be theft."

"The donkey is all I have."

"Nonsense."

"And he has only me. How can I desert him? He trusts me, he licks my face at night."

"Soon you'll tell me that he reads to you from the Psalms!" said Rabbi Yehuda. "It's an animal, a simple animal. You cannot let your fate depend on a donkey."

"The animals were here before us. God gave them preference at Creation."

"And so what?" the rebbe exclaimed. "The plants also existed before us. Should we therefore have a conversation with onions? Do we have to dance the hora with a turnip?"

But no matter how he tried to convince Gershom, the old

man shook his head fiercely. He would stay with the donkey. His decision was made.

What could Rabbi Yehuda do? In order to relieve at least some of his guilt, he pulled off his gabardine coat and dug up the rest of the field. He kept his hat on. And because it is written that we should serve our neighbors with joy, he tried not to think of the midday prayer that he was missing, or of what his wife would say about the dust on his clothes. In shirtsleeves, he toiled until evening fell, while Gershom, seated on a fallen birch tree, watched with admiration and exclaimed: "Not bad for a cobbler, not bad at all!"

For the farmers of Slomniki the month of Mary had come. Every Sunday a procession passed through the hamlet. In front walked four burly fellows with a sedan chair on their shoulders. In it, the statue of the Holy Mother stood on a red velvet pillow. It was freshly painted every year for this occasion. But for generations no one had thought to scrub the fly specks from the statue, so that the Virgin, from the crown on her head to within the folds of her dress, looked pockmarked. This was not out of place, because everyone who was sick in any way whatever trudged in the parade. Behind the young men with incense burners and the priest deep in prayer marched villagers with club feet or water on the brain, with whooping cough and abscesses as well as invisible ailments. Children clasped small bouquets of wilted wildflowers. Black rosaries swayed back and forth in the rough fingers of the women. At the very end hobbled Sam Petscher. His blue hat was pulled down over his eyebrows, and he leaned heavily on Ruchel's thin shoulders.

While the procession crawled through the valley, Gershom was resting in the meadow next to the field. With eyes closed, he heard the tinkling of the Sanctus bells approach and fade away. Afterwards there was no other sound except for the steady chewing of Menachem, who pulled a clump of dandelion and then a thistle from the ground. The animal did not for a moment lose sight of the old man. It grazed around him in ever tightening circles. Finally it sank down next to him. It nipped at Gershom's jacket until Gershom finally stretched out his hand to caress the donkey's white nose.

For hours on end Gershom and his friend sat together in the grass, man and donkey, as equals. The wind rose toward the evening. The sky darkened quickly, as though a giant hand had pushed a lid over the world. At the horizon, where some light still glowed, sounded the drawn-out rumbling of the start of a thunderstorm. "Do you hear that?" said Gershom, getting up. "A herd of donkeys is galloping through the clouds."

Ruchel had renounced Judaism and converted to the religion of the farmers. On the last Sunday of the month of Mary, she had herself baptized along with Sam, who had to be carted into the church on a wheelbarrow. Once the Petschers had accepted the cross, the priest came daily to the house, at Ruchel's urging, to push the host between Sam's lips. He was now incurably ill. After the priest had been bitten more than once on the thumb and forefinger, he began to use a soup spoon, thereby doing violence to Sam as well as to the sacred nature of the act.

Meanwhile the field had been seeded. The earth itself had taken over Gershom's work. "Don't think that you can hang around the house to get in the priest's way!" said Ruchel. "That poor man has enough to do, putting up with one crazy Jew. He's not eager for a second one, nor am I!"

To be rid of Gershom, she gave him the task of cutting willows. From then on he strolled with Menachem to the bank of the river where osiers grew. With trembling fingers he cut off the supple branches. He worked slowly with long breaks. Ever earlier in the afternoon he'd fall asleep at the water's edge. There he dreamed of the Garden of Eden where the Messiah sat enthroned, on his right hand the sun and the planets, on his left hand the moon and the stars. At his feet sat patriarchs and prophets, scholars of Scripture and temple servants, and all the Jews from history. In the crowd he discovered Hanna as well. Her shroud was beaded with rubies. She wore a veil, and she blushed as she had done on the day he stood with her under the marriage canopy.

One time she appeared to him in the middle of the night. Lithe as a young girl, she crouched down next to his straw mattress and kissed his hand.

"Are there donkeys too in the Garden of Eden?" asked

Gershom, whispering for fear that Sam and Ruchel would hear him.

And Hanna, without moving her lips, answered: "There are donkeys and sheep, chickens and dogs, sparrows and beetles, just like here. On the Day of Judgment they will bear witness against humans. They'll testify against every person who has drowned a litter of cats, against every one who has unnecessarily spurred his horses or hurt any animal whatsoever."

"But why didn't I see any animals when I dreamt about the Garden of Eden?"

"Because, like most people, you were blinded by the majesty of the Messiah," said Hanna. "You must pay closer attention next time."

And indeed, the next day when he lay dreaming on the grass, Gershom discovered the animals in a place where he had least expected them. Behind the throne of the Messiah there rose another throne, wide and made of green marble. On its steps crawled and fluttered, chirped and bleated all the creatures that are found on Earth. Past the confusion of wings and tails, his gaze lifted until he found the donkeys. They were standing at the top, and they were all wearing prayer shawls that covered their ears. In the middle of each forehead, there was a golden *shin*, the first letter of the name of God. They brayed loudly, but just when Gershom thought he understood the words that they were speaking in their own language, he woke up, his face covered with sweat.

Fear gripped his heart. What did the dream mean? How could the Messiah allow donkeys to wrap themselves in prayer shawls? And why did He let them wear the name of Shaddai with impunity? Gershom realized that Hanna couldn't possibly have whispered such blasphemous dreams to him. They must be the work of a devil who had taken Hanna's form and who wanted to plunge him into misfortune. To prevent this devil from leading him astray again, he no longer lay down in the grass. He didn't even dare to rest in a sitting position, afraid that his eyes would close unexpectedly. All day long he kept working. And in the evening, when he lay exhausted on his straw mattress, he abandoned himself to sleep with reluctance.

The donkey was restless as well. He brayed more often and longer than usual. He had always adapted his tempo to Gershom's snail's pace, but now he suddenly would run along, disappear from sight, and a little later, snorting loudly, would trot toward the old man. He whipped his tail as though he wanted to swat not only his own flies but those of all of Slomniki as well. He stamped his hooves and reared.

"It's his time," Gershom said to Ruchel. "We have to find a she-ass for him."

"What do you know about that?" said Ruchel mockingly. She had other things on her mind besides a hot-blooded donkey. She had appointed herself the laundress of the priest and was just about to plunge one of his white lace outer garments into a starch bath. "Next week," she said waving him aside, "I'll see about it next week."

Gershom was short of breath. It felt as though there were a knot in his windpipe. On the way to the river he often had to stop in order to catch his breath. And when he bent over too far during the pruning, he burst out in a rasping cough that lasted for minutes. He sighed after one of these coughing fits. "Soon I'll be braying like you." He let his knife rest and turned to Menachem who lifted his head, a mouthful of dandelions between his teeth. Never before had the donkey looked at the old man so directly, from the bottom of his being. Gershom felt small under the gaze of those dark eyes that seemed to contain thousands of years. What secrets had these eyes fathomed? Their memory went back to the time when Abraham was accompanied by donkeys over dusty caravan roads. It was as impossible to imagine Holy Scripture without donkeys as it was without the children of Israel. Donkeys had stood at the foot of Mount Sinai when Moses received the Torah. Donkeys had dragged the stones for building the Temple of Solomon. Throughout history they had kept pace with the Jews, perhaps because the Jewish people, as no other, shared their lot. Weren't both, Jew as well as donkey, outcasts in the world? Hadn't both been ridiculed, hounded, and slaughtered for centuries?

Gershom turned around, brooding, while behind him Menachem began grazing again. Yes, everything was becoming clear to the old man. Jews were the donkeys among people, and donkeys were the Jews among animals. He now understood why the donkeys in the Garden of Eden wore prayer shawls with the permission of the Messiah. In his imagination, the Messiah himself became a donkey, followed by a vast herd that would advance to Jerusalem in a storming gallop in order to bring peace and justice to humanity and to restore the Kingdom of David to its glory.

On impulse he threw back his head. He bared his upper teeth and, panting, pumped air into his lungs the way he had often seen Menachem do. Then Gershom Katz brayed triumphantly and freely, as though he had never done anything else during his whole long life. He heard the donkey respond, and he heard his hooves stamping. But before he could turn around, the donkey had jumped on his back. With the impact of a sledgehammer Gershom was thrown to the ground. The knife slipped out of his hand.

At twilight the pair was found by playing children. Half the village came out to look. The donkey had clamped his front legs around Gershom's shoulders, and in that embrace they had crashed forward together. Neither the man nor the animal had been able to free himself. Gershom must have collapsed under the weight almost immediately, for his face, turned aside as though he had looked back at the donkey during his fall, had a smile. The donkey, whose front legs had been broken, was still alive. It didn't move, but when Rabbi Yehuda kneeled and closed Gershom's eyes, it made a vain attempt to bite him.

Months later, in the streets and in the markets of Slomniki, to anyone who didn't know yet and to anyone who never tired of hearing it, the story would be told of how the donkey, with upper lip drawn and trembling nostrils, remained lying down until Yankel the butcher appeared, how Yankel then had crushed the animal's skull with a hammer, and how in the end five men had been needed to free Gershom's body from the grip of his lover.

While the hide of the donkey was drying in the sun, Gershom Katz was escorted to his grave by a procession of villagers. Sam Petscher and his wife Ruchel were not among those who said Kaddish for him. Their voices were not heard among the many voices that intoned the farewell prayer for the dead, whose echo was blown over the crooked, sagging tombstones by a summer breeze.

> *All-powerful king, you*
> *who support whoever stumbles,*
> *liberate whoever is in shackles—*
> *no one is like you*
> *you who celebrate the word*
> *and will bring to life once again*
> *he who slumbers here deep in the earth.*

HOLY FIRE

T HIS IS THE STORY OF HANS LEVIE AND THE TRANS-
formation that he underwent. Although it was not as
spectacular as the metamorphosis of Gregor Samsa, who,
according to Kafka, awoke one morning as a monstrous cock-
roach, to this day Hans's parents have not recovered from their
fright, and maybe they never will.

Through my long friendship with his mother, Miriam, I
have watched Hans grow up, from his first steps to his first
bicycle, from nursery school to high school. I also spent several
summer vacations with the Levies in Brittany, but what I
remember most about those is the view of the windy beach and
the sea, with Hans in the distant background, hanging onto a
kite or up to his waist in a sandy hole. When he was sixteen,

just before his life took a disastrous turn, Hans was an average boy with blond hair and rosy cheeks, dividing his attention between soccer and girls. He wasn't very clever. The postcards and the few letters from him that I have saved bristle with errors. Was I fond of him? I know only that I didn't find him particularly objectionable. I was rather indifferent to him. In retrospect I think that's unfortunate. If I'd paid more attention to him at the time, maybe now I'd be able to give an explanation, any explanation whatsoever, for his later behavior. But he wasn't the kind of boy who inspires curiosity. And anyway, perhaps it's an illusion that we, who understand so little about ourselves, can truly fathom what possesses others.

I met Miriam in 1971. One evening in February she showed up at my door, very pregnant and rain-drenched. She had, she explained, searched the local telephone directory page by page for Jewish last names, and now she was dropping in on those people, hoping to interest them in getting together.

"Getting together?" I asked suspiciously. "To do what?"

"To exchange ideas with kindred spirits. With people to whom you don't have to explain anything and from whom you don't have to hide anything. And to whom you can tell your best Jewish joke with confidence." She made this speech as though she'd practiced it at home.

"My best Jewish joke? I'm no good at telling jokes."

"How do you like this one?" she said. "Jake says to Sam that he wants to be baptized. What a disgrace, says Sam, your father will turn over in his grave. Says Jake: That's all right, my brother is getting baptized next week, and then father will be on his back again."

I waved my hand; I knew a much better one.

Laughing, we walked to the kitchen, and before long we were engaged in a passionate discussion about ginger shortbread, herring salad, and books by Bernard Malamud.

The first meeting was held in Miriam and her husband Alex's house. They had just moved in. Amidst the chaos of the enclosed porch, where cardboard boxes were stacked everywhere, those present shyly sat together while a parrot screeched: "Hello, raisin bun; hello, raisin bun." We were six, including the host and hostess. The idea was for all of us to introduce ourselves and then briefly say something about our past.

There was Thérèse Twersky, in her early fifties, originally French, a potter, elegant and lively. She said that she didn't actually know why she had accepted Miriam's invitation. She was only moderately interested in Judaism. But she was fascinated by Buddhism and by other exotic religions. She had just returned from a trip to Mexico where, searching for inspiration, she had studied classic Native American ceramics. When she spoke at too great length about the differences between Olmec, Zapotec, Chichimik, and Aztec pottery, Miriam firmly took over.

Then there were Isidore Galatzer and his wife Rose, both

short, stocky, originally from Romania. They were the same age as Thérèse. Rose was in a wheelchair. A result of the war, she explained. She'd been imprisoned in Vertujen, a Romanian concentration camp where the only food was a cattle feed that caused gradual paralysis. Upon liberation she'd had to leave the camp by crawling on her knees. She'd lost all strength in her leg muscles. In addition she could barely move her left arm.

"Compared to Vertujen," she said, "Auschwitz was a vacation spot."

"Oh, really," said Thérèse indignantly. "If I'd only known sooner. I would have taken along my bathing suit and suntan cream."

"Were you in Auschwitz?" Miriam asked.

Thérèse nodded.

"At least you got some bread," said Isidore to Thérèse. "We got absolutely nothing. The Romanians didn't need the Germans to get rid of the Jews. They did it themselves; they did it on Romanian soil and as cheaply as possible. Trains, gas chambers, bread rations—they thought that was money down the drain. Jews weren't even worth kicking to death. We had to be destroyed, but without costing a cent. They made us walk enormous distances. Whoever didn't collapse from exhaustion on the way would starve later in the camp. I was imprisoned in Dumanovka. There, we ate grass. But I escaped. For a year I hid in the forests. Underground, like a rat in a hole. I almost went crazy."

"Isidore hates anything that's Romanian," said Rose. "He doesn't even allow me to sing Romanian songs."

"The only good Romanian is a dead Romanian," shouted Isidore, his face red with excitement. "There wasn't one Romanian who helped me, not one."

Thérèse kept silent, and I stared into my coffee cup.

Miriam, who saw her carefully prepared evening beginning to fall apart, gathered all her courage. "I was *most certainly* helped," she said with emphasis. "By a miner's family in Limburg. With nine children. I was hidden there until the end of the war. They lived in a small, dilapidated house, and they all slept in the attic. I was four years old and had lived in an enormous mansion in the Hague. So when I stepped over the threshold in Limburg, the first thing I exclaimed was: Where is the sofa? Where is the piano?"

We laughed, all except Isidore. Sighing, he loosened his tie and undid the collar of his shirt.

"They were sweet people," said Miriam, "They had no fear. In the village I went to school normally, supposedly as their niece from a northern province. For my own protection they taught me to say the Hail Mary. I still know it."

Speaking more to herself than to us, she began in a singsong voice: "Hail Mary, full of Grace, the Lord be with you…"

"Hello, raisin bun," the parrot shouted irreverently.

"I get enticed to come here under the pretense of a Jewish gathering," muttered Isidore, "and then they recite the Hail Mary."

Relieved, everyone started talking at once. Alex threw me an understanding look across the table. We were the only ones who hadn't said a word yet.

I soon became attached to our little group assembled by chance from the telephone book. Alex and Miriam, Isidore and Rose, Thérèse and I were the faithful ones from the very beginning. In those early days an alliance was established among us that remained indestructible through the years, even after our numbers increased and we got membership administration and bookkeeping, our own house of prayer, a cantor, and a part-time rabbi.

Alex took on the task of secretary. Miriam and Thérèse started to learn Hebrew and soon became quite proficient. Isidore became treasurer, while Rose, using only one hand, embroidered a beautiful mantle for the brand-new Torah scroll. But I kept apart. I rarely showed up in the synagogue. The services lasted too long, and even though I tried to let myself be carried away by the prayers, they never became more than protocol for me. Once in a while, on holidays, I would go anyway, but chiefly to nestle next to Thérèse and to enjoy the intimacy of our leafing together through one prayer book. Or to experience one of the few occasions when Isidore pressed against his wife's wheelchair and spread his prayer shawl over her head and his own. At that moment they seemed like normal people who had never heard of Vertujen or Dumanovka. Under the white silk tallit they looked as delighted as children who under the covers tell each other their deepest secrets and who peek out from between the sheets only to make sure that no one is eavesdropping.

None of them blamed me for not attending the services and the meetings regularly.

"You aren't suited for organization life," Miriam said with a certain tenderness. "That's hardly a crime, is it?"

Isidore was even proud of what he called my independence. "If you ever have to sit in a pit in the woods, you'll stay completely sane." He nodded contentedly. "You don't need anyone, you'll manage quite well."

The truth was that I wouldn't have known what to do without them. I have never felt at home anywhere the way I did with them. I'm not easy on myself and certainly not on others. They knew how to love me and, what's more, to do so effortlessly.

A few weeks after Hans's sixteenth birthday, Miriam called me. She asked me whether I was interested in a lecture about Solomon Ibn Gabirol. She explained that Gabirol was a Jewish scholar from the Spanish Middle Ages, and that he had written poems that had become part of the service.

"Next week, Sunday," she said, "in Amsterdam. It starts at two o'clock in the afternoon, so we have to leave here at noon."

Then she lowered her voice.

"Do you know that Hans is no longer going to school? He's

already been at home for four days. I have to speak softly, because he's walking around here somewhere."

"Cutting school happens in the best families," I said.

"No, it's not cutting school. He's refusing to stay in that school. He says that it's a stupid, provincial school for farmhands. He complains that we've moved to Groningen where he now has to waste his life. How could you have done that to me? he says. As if we are in the middle of the Sahara or the jungle."

"Is he having problems with a teacher or something?"

"I thought so at first, but I called the school, and there's nothing wrong. No, it's much deeper. He feels that this isn't a city for Jews. There's no Yiddishkeit here, he says."

"Hans and Yiddishkeit?" I laughed. "Since when does he worry about Yiddishkeit? He doesn't even know the difference between Abraham and Moses."

"I don't understand it either. In the beginning I thought: Don't worry, it's adolescence, others suffer from acne and your son suffers from Yiddishkeit. But he's dead serious. He's suddenly brought home all sorts of books about Judaism."

"Brought home? Don't you already have enough books about it?"

"No, he doesn't think much of our books. They're too liberal for him."

"It's hard to believe. Especially since he always disliked religion so much."

"Yes, I know, he never wanted anything to do with it. He wanted to be like the other children in his class. How often did he pester me about a Christmas tree and Easter eggs? On Saturdays, when we went to the Sabbath service, he went to the soccer field. We always let him do whatever he liked. And now this."

"What does Alex think of it?"

"You know Alex. He has no patience at all for these things. In the evening he comes home from work dead tired and pushes everything off on me. Yesterday he said: 'You give in too easily. Be firm and send that boy back to school.'"

There was silence for a moment. She heaved a big sigh.

"I don't know," she said. "Maybe he's right. I did become a mother very late in life."

"Nonsense," I said. "That's typically female. A man looks at us with reproach, and we go and stand in the corner of our own free will. Women have an overdeveloped sense of guilt. Why doesn't *Alex* stand firm? Why doesn't *Alex* send Hans back to school? Isn't Hans his son too?"

"Yes, but Hans won't have anything to do with his old school. He just wants to go to a Jewish school."

"Then he's out of luck. There are no Jewish schools in this city."

"He's made calls to schools in Antwerp and Amsterdam."

"But how can he go there? He has his final examinations next year. For sixteen years he didn't care about Yiddishkeit, so it can't be terribly urgent. Maybe it will pass. Let him finish the school year."

The tone of Miriam's voice changed. "That's settled then," she said cheerfully. "You're going with us to Amsterdam. Thérèse is also coming. Rose is still considering; she's always afraid to be a bother to others with her wheelchair."

"Is Hans around?" I asked, whispering in spite of myself.

"Yes," she exclaimed, "I'll take care of transportation. Alex can easily do without the car for an evening."

"Good," I said, "we'll discuss this another time. We should definitely talk about it again."

But she had already hung up with a quick goodbye.

In the afternoon I bicycled to Thérèse's studio. Although almost seventy, she still worked every day. She was at the potter's wheel in the back of the room, her gray hair down her back in a careless braid. I liked to watch while under her hands pots and pitchers made their shining pirouettes.

"*Ma petite*," she said without looking up.

"Am I interrupting?"

"*Pas du tout*." She stopped the wheel. "It's not working today."

She went to wash up at the sink and took off her apron.

"It's always something nowadays," she said. "If it isn't my shoulders, then it's my back. Souvenirs of Auschwitz."

With disdain, she looked at the bowl she had made.

"See, I create all new things. But I myself am cracked."

Still, she seemed amazingly intact for someone her age. She possessed the tough flexibility of a ballerina. In the most shapeless sweater she appeared distinguished.

Together we stood in front of the window. She pointed to the crown of a tall maple in which the outline of a dome-shaped nest was visible.

"That belongs to two magpies," she said. "They build their nest with a roof, just like us, and they coat it with mud. A few months ago, when there was such a terrible storm, the whole nest fell down. The next morning they began all over again, twig by twig."

She put her arm around me

"When it all becomes too much for me," she said, "I look at that nest. Then I tell myself that I should be like the magpies. That I should live from day to day and do my work. Not look into the abyss but continue. Just continue until the next storm."

We drank some coffee.

I asked her if she had heard that Hans was troubled by attacks of Yiddishkeit.

She knew about it but thought the matter hardly worth discussing. "A symptom of adolescence," she said with a nonchalant wave of her hand. "He's sixteen and wants to drive his parents up the wall."

"Well, then, he's succeeded," I said. "When Miriam called

me this morning, she sounded very unhappy. She thinks she's failed as a mother."

Thérèse yawned.

"That's part of it," she said. "Did Miriam say anything to you about the lecture?"

I nodded.

"I promised that I'd come along," I said, "but I don't really feel like it."

"You don't feel like it?" she exclaimed. "It's a great opportunity. The lecturer is Benjamin Lemberg. A fantastic man and an authority. There is no one who knows as much about the Jewish poets of Spain as Lemberg. He's devoted his whole life to the subject."

"Yes, but he's coming to talk only about Gabirol. I'd rather hear something about others. About Ha-Nagid, for example."

Thérèse, who didn't consider me qualified to express opinions about these matters, shrugged her shoulders patronizingly.

"Why Ha-Nagid?"

"Because he was practically everything at once. Philosopher and linguist, rabbi and poet. As vizier to the Caliph of Granada, he became commander of the royal forces. A Jew at the head of an Islamic army—that speaks to my imagination. Twenty long years he fought. He won one battle after the other. You wonder how with all that din of clashing arms he found time for writing. Still, he wrote the most beautiful poetry."

Enthusiastically, I recited:

> *Be brave in times of danger or sorrow,*
> *even when standing at death's door.*
> *A lamp glows brightest before the morrow.*
> *Lions when wounded loudest roar.*

"That certainly is beautiful," Thérèse admitted. "Where did you get that translation?"

My face flushed. "It's mine."

"Since when do you know Hebrew?"

"I learned it as a child."

"Why didn't you tell us?"

"I don't know. Maybe because I was afraid that you'd expect all sorts of things from me."

"So while we took you for an illiterate, you sat at home, secretly translating Ha-Nagid?"

"Promise not to tell the others," I said.

"Do you also read the Torah?"

"That too," I said reluctantly. "But don't misunderstand. I do it only because I like the sound of the language and the metaphors."

"You don't need to make excuses," said Thérèse. "Reading the Torah is not a punishable offense. The age of the Inquisition is past."

"I'm not making excuses at all. Why should I?"

"You yourself know that best, *ma petite*. Someone who translates Ha-Nagid isn't exactly stupid."

In fact, I did possess an excellent knowledge of the Torah and related matters, which I had concealed from the others in our group. My intention was to avoid the long prayer services and the joint study of Scripture, but mostly I didn't want to be reminded of my past.

I grew up in an Orthodox family in Antwerp. My father, a pious Jew who earned his living by teaching Hebrew and the Talmud, dreamed of progeny consisting of nothing but rabbis and cantors. He would have preferred to raise twelve sons, like Jacob. When my mother, after several miscarriages, presented him with only one daughter, he could hardly swallow his disappointment. All his paternal ambition was concentrated on me. Evening after evening I sat bent over books from which he instructed me in the reading and explication of Holy Scripture.

Outside the house I was timid and awkward. I understood practically nothing about the world and its ways. Whatever I knew, I had taught myself and learned in secret. From the school library I took home novels in which there was not a word about God. In modern magazines I read articles about love, sexuality, and other matters that were barely mentioned in the Torah. Girlfriends in my classes listened to records by the Beatles and the Rolling Stones, uninhibited boys in tight pants who called things by their true names. Whereas in Genesis it says covertly, "And he came to her," they sang openly: "Treat me like you did the night before," and "I can't get no satisfaction."

For my father, worldly matters didn't seem to exist. His whole life, including the smallest everyday thing, was directed toward God. Judaism has prayers for almost everything—for bread and other food, for smells, colors, and sounds. My father used them all. He did that "because all that we enjoy here on Earth is a gift from the Almighty, and therefore every pleasure, no matter how small, loses its value for us if we do not honor our Creator for it." He praised God for the taste of fresh coffee and for the chirping of innocent sparrows on the windowsill. He even said a blessing over the inkpot from which he filled his pen. Until deep into the night he sat bent over the *Guide for the Perplexed*, the *Source of Life*, and other mystical texts.

He took almost every word from the holy books literally. In this he went so far that he considered the Earth as the center of the universe. Although even imbeciles had been convinced of the contrary for centuries, he maintained that the sun turned around the Earth. He had established a society that, in addition to himself, had three members: a partially deaf neighbor, our kosher baker, and a retired fur dealer, all of whom frequented the same house of prayer as my father and upon whom he had imposed his eccentric point of view. They called themselves the Brothers of Gibeon, after the place where, according to Scripture, the sun had stopped in the sky for a whole day at the command of Joshua. The meetings that the society held in our living room were noisy. My father always gave a long speech. He did that standing up while taking small, tripping steps like a boxer in the ring. His body swayed as though he were praying, and under the coat of his black suit the white fringes of his prayer shirt began to tremble. His movements seemed threatening, like those of a boxer in the ring. Everything on him was in turmoil—even his glasses kept sliding to the tip of his nose. He quoted patriarchs, prophets, and kabbalists, anyone who had written anything that suited his beliefs about the heavenly bodies. He let his voice surge to unprecedented volume, perhaps because he feared that his listeners, all being gentlemen of a certain age, would doze off.

My mother had reconciled herself to the existence of this crazy club, but my own opposition to it grew as I became older.

"You don't really think that the sun revolves around the Earth?" I said to my father.

"I don't think so," he answered, "I know it for sure."

"And Kepler? And Galileo?"

"They were totally off the mark."

"You sound so certain—as if they were carpenters or iron-mongers."

"That's probably true."

"And Newton?"

"What do you mean, Newton?" my father exclaimed vehemently. "I'm referring to texts that are thousands of years old.

That Newton of yours is only a toddler compared to them, an insignificant nincompoop."

The gulf between my father and me constantly grew wider. On my eighteenth birthday, when I told him that I wanted to become a journalist, the bomb exploded. He had hoped that I would marry, preferably Benjamin Kirschner, one of his students who clutched a prayer book to his chest wherever he went and who blushed when he met me. But my father realized that no God-fearing man would want to stand under the marriage canopy with a future journalist, and conversely, that no journalist would want to share her life with someone whose idea of the latest news was medieval Bible commentaries. After a terrible fight I left the house for good. Alone, on a rented delivery bicycle loaded with bags and boxes, I disappeared from the sight of my weeping mother. At that moment the chances of my father's having a rabbi as son-in-law evaporated. He never forgave me.

At my departure he cursed me from the bottom of his heart. He shouted at me, telling me that I was an ungrateful bitch and that outside the safety of the family I would amount to nothing. But he was as mistaken in this as he was in the movements of the heavenly bodies. I found a job at the *Northern Daily* in Groningen, where, after an internship, I got a permanent job on the national and foreign affairs editorial staff.

At first I kept in touch with my mother, but our infrequent correspondence soon came to an end. My father had sprinkled ashes on his head and said Kaddish, the traditional prayer for the dead, for me. I no longer existed for him, I had become a spirit. He wouldn't allow my mother to keep in touch with me and he referred to Leviticus, in which the God of Israel says: *And if any person turns to ghosts and familiar spirits and goes astray after them, I will set My face against that person and cut him off from among his people.* That scared my mother thoroughly.

The last sign of life that I received from her was a parcel. It contained an old book, without a spine and spattered with grease. On the cover it said in worn gold letters: *Ritual Cookbook.* When I opened it, a note in her neat, sloping handwriting fell out. She wrote that she had waited for years to give me this book, which had belonged to my grandmother. Now, to her unspeakable sadness, she was obliged to send it to me as a goodbye. She wished me much luck with it and referred to page 151 for my favorite dish, kugel with pears.

The pages were tattered. The book had been published in 1932 under the supervision of two rabbis, an urologist, and a specialist in stomach, intestinal, and metabolic diseases. It contained references to Creation and to the Flood. Users of this book could not fry an egg without being reminded of the dangers of idolatry, murder, and lawlessness. The writers, the ladies Glück and Bramson, urged over and over again the strict observance of dietary laws and warned of spiritual degeneration. Was that the reason my mother had sent me the book? Did she hope to protect me from degeneration? As though the events after 1932 hadn't shown that there exists a degeneration that won't be restrained by anything or anyone, not by religious leaders or politicians and certainly not by a cookbook. The thought was almost touching in its innocence. I imagined the newspaper headlines: *The ladies Glück and Bramson cause the fall of the Third Reich. Jewish cookbook compulsory reading for Germans. Adolf Hitler defeated by kugel with pears.*

This was how matters stood. My father had declared me dead, and my mother, albeit reluctantly, had followed him in this. They had banished their daughter to the realm of the spirits. And as the years passed, they in turn became increasingly like spirits for me. What should I tell Alex, Miriam, and the others about my parents? We had cut ourselves off from each other.

During our outing to Amsterdam, Miriam was deliberately cheerful. She didn't mention Hans. And either because we didn't want to spoil the mood or because of cowardice, we avoided asking about him.

But in the months that followed, his name came up often, usually when anything changed in Miriam and Alex's household. Like the time we noticed they had gotten a new tea set.

"Lovely," I said.

"Pretty, those yellow flowers," said Rose holding her cup up to the light.

But Thérèse, who had personally created the old tea service, asked, "What's wrong with the other one? Are you tired of it?"

"Well," said Miriam, avoiding Thérèse's eyes, "I wanted something different."

But later, when the subject of the discussion had changed, Miriam suddenly exclaimed: "It was washed away."

We didn't understand what she was talking about.

"Thérèse's tea set," explained Miriam. "I'd rather tell the truth. It was washed away."

"That doesn't surprise me at all," said Rose. "That dishwasher of yours has been making such strange noises."

"No," said Miriam, pointing toward the garden doors, "it washed away in the canal in back. It's because of Hans. He said that my dishes were not kosher and that I had to clean them."

"Clean them?" I asked disbelieving. "In that canal? That's where the dirtiest factories discharge their waste products."

Miriam looked helpless. "He said that I had to immerse them in naturally running water. And the canal is the only naturally running water in the area. So I went there carrying bags filled with dishes, near the lock where the current is strongest."

"You must be crazy," said Thérèse.

"I did it because otherwise he wouldn't eat at home anymore. And we see so little of him as it is."

Meanwhile Hans was living in Antwerp, where he was completing high school in a strict religious school. He was boarding with a Hasidic family. Because his religious conviction made it impossible for him to travel on the Sabbath, and because he had lessons on Sunday as well, he spent only his vacations at home.

"Was anything else washed away?" asked Thérèse.

"Not the pans," answered Miriam, "because they have handles. But almost everything else, including the knives and forks. Alex was angry with Hans, but Hans said that it was our own fault. 'Can I help it,' he said, 'that you live like unbelievers? You don't even know the simplest rules. If you lived in Antwerp, you wouldn't have these problems. Then the dishes wouldn't be lying at the bottom of the canal!' "

"And these new dishes?" worried Rose, as she inspected the contents of her cup. "Did you clean them in the canal as well?"

"I don't dare to anymore. We've found another solution. Hans brought pots with him that were cleaned in Antwerp under rabbinical supervision. He prepares his own meals in those, on an electric hot plate in his room. And he eats from plastic plates."

"Mon Dieu!" sighed Thérèse.

"Why do you give in to him in such idiotic things?" I wanted to know.

Feeling uneasy because of our vehement reactions, Miriam tightened her face. "I want to respect his views," she said stiffly. "Frederick the Great said that everyone must find salvation in his own way. *Jeder soll selig werden nach seiner Façon.* And I completely agree with him."

"Oh, la la," said Thérèse. "I didn't know that we'd be having tea with Frederick the Great."

"Is he kosher enough?" I teased. "Shouldn't you ask Hans's approval?"

"Which Frederick?" asked Rose, slow to understand as always.

We were all speaking at the same time.

Miriam shouted over everything: "You can say what you want, but I admire Hans. I admire his self-discipline. He used to be too damned lazy to sit and do his homework for even an hour. Now he can't get enough of it. All day long he's with his books, from early morning till late at night. It's hard work to be a good Jew, you can take that from me. He sacrifices everything for it."

"Even his own father and mother," snapped Thérèse.

"You don't understand," said Miriam. "It's as difficult for him as it is for us. He would rather just eat from my plates. But he can't do that; it goes against his principles."

"A sixteen-year-old who from one day to the next acquires holy principles and tyrannizes everyone around him with them?" said Thérèse. *"Je m'en fous."*

"Hans has enormous dedication," Miriam said emphatically, perhaps to overcome her own doubts. "A dedication that you seldom find nowadays. His ideas on Judaism don't necessarily match ours, but at any rate he lives according to them. Many people could follow his example."

At these last words she looked at me sideways.

Dejected, we were silent. Some minutes passed.

Rose, who had only half understood, tried to get the conversation going again.

"Nice dishes," she said awkwardly, "So sunny, with those yellow flowers."

Miriam rubbed her face wearily.

"You think so? Well, it's a change."

We had expected that Alex, being sarcastic and inflexible, would bring Hans in line. But that didn't happen. To our great amazement Alex became only more accommodating. Perhaps he didn't want to spoil the little time that Hans spent at home by having fights, which might alienate the boy even further. Perhaps he feared resistance from Miriam, who was plagued by guilt feelings and ready to give in to the boy in everything. But he probably thought, as we did, that Hans's Yiddishkeit was nothing more than a way to rebel against his parents. After all, what did Isidore, Rose, Thérèse, and I know about children? Because we ourselves were childless, we withheld our judgment of those who had been bold enough to have them.

But we weren't blind. And although we joked about it among ourselves, it was not without concern that we noticed how rapidly the strict mores that Hans learned in Antwerp took over the parental home. At his urging, a mezuzah appeared on almost every doorpost. At his urging, the walls were purged of all images that were offensive to Orthodox notions, so that most paintings were banished to the attic. At his urging, Miriam started wearing clothes that covered her arms below the elbows and her legs below the knees. At his urging, Alex gave up drinking whiskey and got rid of his wine cellar. At every meeting we saw the compelling hand of Hans. Had the magazines on the coffee table been replaced by a massive reference work about Jewish ethics? Hans must be behind that. Did an enormous eight-branched candelabrum appear in the windowsill? Hans must have placed it there. Isidore, Rose, Thérèse, and I silently threw each other glances in which the same word could be read every time: *Hans, Hans, Hans*.

Finally even the parrot disappeared.

"Where did Yupi go?" asked Isidore, shocked, during one of our get-togethers.

He was standing in the enclosed porch in the place where the cage had been for years. The hand he had lifted to scratch the parrot's neck between the feathers dropped limply.

Alex squirmed with embarrassment.

"Hmm, Yupi," he said, surprised, as though he hadn't noticed the absence of the parrot before this.

Miriam came to his rescue.

"Yupi was annoying," she said. "Every time Hans started his afternoon prayer, Yupi would screech through it. You know what a racket he could make. Not a sensible word came out. All day long it was: 'Hello, raisin bun; hello, raisin bun.'"

• 64 •

She laughed, but Isidore stiffened.

"You're not going to tell me that you got rid of Yupi?"

"We didn't get rid of him," said Alex. "We found him a home with a real fancier, someone with five other parrots and a cockatoo."

"Wait a minute," said Isidore, "this is beyond me. Yupi has always made a racket, as long as I've been coming to your house. And suddenly, because the animal can't pray, he has to disappear?"

"Yupi was a difficult case," said Miriam. "We couldn't figure out whether he was an unclean bird, but Hans had his suspicions. The Talmud says nothing about parrots, but with that curved beak and those claws on their legs, they resemble birds of prey. And birds of prey are not allowed."

"Are not allowed by whom?" Isidore exclaimed angrily.

"By the rabbinate."

"Perhaps *eating* parrots is forbidden," said Isidore, "but you're still allowed to keep them as pets."

"That's permitted, but Hans says that it isn't wise to surround yourself with unclean animals."

Isidore's eyes filled with tears. "But didn't God create these animals Himself? If Hans can do it better, why doesn't he organize his own creation, somewhere in a remote spot? A world for him alone, without parrots. And also without his father and mother, because they no longer seem to be able to do anything right in his eyes."

"What are you saying?" Alex shouted, agitated.

"Oh, please," hushed Miriam.

"No," Alex said bitterly. "No, he's going too far. He shouldn't interfere with our family life. This is my house, and I'm the boss here. What I do with my parrot or with my son is none of his damned business!"

Isidore gasped for breath.

"Don't get excited," whispered Rose. "Please, think of your heart."

Thérèse, to restore the peace, asked the quarreling parties to sit down and count to one hundred. But Isidore shook his head.

"I wish you had given Yupi to us," he said regretfully as he pushed the wheelchair with Rose in it away. "We thought he was a sweet bird. We would have liked to take him home. For that we don't have to consult the rabbinate, not us."

Without saying goodbye he left the house with his wife. It was the first time that our group had been divided by a quarrel.

Since Hans had gone to live in Antwerp we hadn't seen him at all. That could hardly be accidental. I suspected that Alex and Miriam had arranged it that way. Whenever Hans spent a vacation in Holland, they scrupulously kept Rose, Isidore, Thérèse, and me away from their house. Were they afraid that their son would be offended by our liberal behavior? Or did they worry that we would be chased away by his pious talk? They obviously thought nothing good could come from a confrontation, and they were probably right.

Even when he finished high school, we didn't get to see Hans. In the summer, after he had passed his final examinations, he left for New York. He had enrolled in an institute for Talmudic studies in Brooklyn. Miriam glowed with pride. On the Sabbath after his departure, she came up to us in the synagogue. The service was over. We stood around talking over a cup of coffee.

"Did you hear?" she asked triumphantly. "Hans is studying in America now."

We congratulated her warmly.

"He already has quite a few friends over there," she told us, "because he's joined Chabad."

"He joined what?" asked Rose.

"Chabad," repeated Miriam.

"A Hasidic sect," I said, "that goes into the streets in buses to bring disaffected Jews back to the faith."

"It's not a sect," said Miriam, offended, "it's a movement."

I shrugged my shoulders. "A sect or a movement, it all comes down to the same thing."

"They're two very different things," Miriam said, piqued.

"At any rate," I said, continuing my explanation to Rose, "an ancient rabbi is at the head of it. His name is Menachem Mendel Schneerson and he has proclaimed himself prophet or Messiah, or both. He has visions and he makes predictions. Some say he's holy. Others, like me, think that he's a charlatan."

Miriam protested. "Schneerson has already cured thousands of sick with his prayers!"

"Yes," I said, "he performs healing work for humanity, but he doesn't do it for nothing. He expects to be paid for each prayer."

"Why does that matter?" said Miriam. "Don't doctors ask money for a treatment?"

I nodded. "Of course. But a doctor has had training. Schneerson is unqualified."

"He doesn't need training," she said, "because he is a seer. His knowledge is innate. He seems to be a descendant of King David."

I burst out laughing. "That's a well-known trick. In Jewish history there have been droves of false prophets and Messiahs. One passed himself off as Moses, another one claimed that he was Daniel or Elijah. They were braggarts and swindlers who had delusions of grandeur. Everywhere they spread stories about their so-called superhuman powers, until they themselves started believing them. Most died a violent death, just like Christ, who is also supposed to be descended directly from King David."

"That's possible," said Miriam, "but does it mean that Schneerson is a swindler? He has followers all over the world."

"A following is not proof of reliability. Every false messiah has followers. Some have had millions. Joseph Stalin, Adolf Hitler, Mao Zedong."

"Yes, if that's how you think!" she said, offended. She turned away and joined another group.

Rose moved restlessly in her wheelchair.

"I don't understand it at all," she said. "Is that Sneepson a rabbi or a doctor?"

Isidore repeated, partly in Romanian, partly in Yiddish, what we had said.

"Well, it won't come to that," said Thérèse. "Hans is a Dutch boy. He is much too sensible to let himself be carried away by a clairvoyant messiah. I've lived in this country for twenty years, and I've never yet seen anyone be carried away. *Ils sont trop flegmatiques, les Néerlandais.* They don't have strong feelings. That is their weakness and their strength."

Isidore said in a muffled voice: "Good riddance. Let him stay in New York, then he can't upset Alex and Miriam."

Rose looked worried. "And what if you're all wrong?" she said. "What if that Sneepson turns out to be the Messiah?"

"We'll be able to tell without any problem," said Thérèse, mockingly, "from the sound of the trumpets."

"And the wolf shall lie down with the lamb," I declared. "And a child shall stretch out his hand over the eye of a viper."

"I'll drink to that," said Isidore as he tossed down his last sip of coffee.

* * *

Not long after that, I received in my mail a letter that appeared to come from Hans. In his almost illegible writing he urged me to hasten the coming of the Messiah. I could do this, he wrote in a childish and sloppy Dutch, by not smoking cigarettes, by not drinking, and by sanctifying the Sabbath. He reminded me that I belonged to a people with a task, who must enlighten the world, a people who has produced thinkers like Spinoza, Freud, Einstein, and many others, mentioning one after the other by their full names, so that his letter resembled a page from the telephone book.

I felt offended, not so much by the message but by the arrogance of the messenger. Who did this conceited adolescent think he was? My response was short but scathing. I opened with a quote from Franz Kafka: *The Messiah will come only when he is no longer needed, he will only come one day after his arrival, he will not come on the last day but on the very last.*

Underneath it I wrote that the Jewish people had indeed produced impressive thinkers but that someone like Hans, who couldn't even spell their names correctly, was hardly justified in feeling related to them, let alone in boasting of such a relationship. "It's true," I wrote, "that the world can use some more light. But not all Jews carry a torch, just as not all torchbearers are Jewish." I was going to mention the names of Erasmus, Dante, and so on, down to Chekhov, but I changed my mind. From one of my desk drawers I dug up a few twenty-dollar bills, which I enclosed with my letter. "Do something nice with the money," I advised him in a postscript. "Have you seen the new Woody Allen film yet?"

Later, Miriam said that Hans had been hurt by my letter because I had quoted a *German* writer. Apparently he was unaware of the fact that Franz Kafka had lived in Prague and was one of the thinkers, according to him, on whom Jewish history possesses an exclusive patent. Miriam also told me that he had spent my dollars on gas to fill up the tank of the van he used to roam the streets of New York, looking for converts. I had financed the missionary work of Schneerson.

Hans stayed in the United States during the whole winter and the following spring. He no longer sent me moralizing letters, but, as befits a good missionary, he didn't lose heart after only one attempt. He gave me ample opportunity to save my immortal soul. With a certain regularity I received English-language magazines and colorful flyers. I never let him know that they had reached me, but I did read them. They were curious propaganda leaflets. We were living, the writers claimed over and over again, in an age of sin and destruction. Creation was thoroughly corrupt. Everywhere in the world people were engaged in slandering, whoring, and cutting each other's throats to their hearts' content, although the Almighty had expressly forbidden this. Fortunately the great change was in sight. The end of time was nearing, Mashiach was preparing to establish the kingdom of David on Earth and to rebuild the destroyed Temple. A horrible fate awaited sinners who did not repent in time. Women would be afflicted by scabies, men would be felled by the sword, and if that weren't sufficient then they all would be consumed by flames.

The illustrations looked familiar to me. Not only were they hardly distinguishable from the pictures in the magazine of the Jehovah's Witnesses, but they also looked suspiciously like the illustrations on book covers and posters of Hitler's time. Stiffly drawn men and women, impeccably dressed and with their hair still wet from their baths, resolutely turned their eyes to the heavens. *We have placed our hope in the Lord. Führer, wir folgen.*

Sometime in June Miriam called me. She was exuberant, like a young girl.

"Hans is coming home next week," she said happily, "and to share his knowledge with others, he wants to invite all of you. Are you free on Thursday evening?"

I had no desire to share the knowledge in question, but I didn't want to offend Miriam. She was my friend, after all. And Hans, however pretentious, was the son of this friend. I therefore promised that I would come, although I had to find a colleague on the national and foreign affairs editorial staff who would be willing to exchange my evening shift for his day shift.

The following Thursday when I arrived at Alex and Miriam's house, I had difficulty finding a parking place. Cars were parked everywhere, on the street and on the sidewalk. Half of the Jewish community was packed into the living room. At the very back of the room, Hans was handing out booklets that were lying in stacks on the closed piano lid. He had become taller and much thinner. Instead of the jeans he used to live in, he now wore a black suit that was too big for him. As I pushed my way toward Hans, I shook hands left and right, greeting friends.

"How are you?"

"Fine."

"How are you two?"

"Fine, fine."

It surprised me to encounter so much contentment, since we at the *Northern Daily* received such avalanches of bad news that we could have filled ten editions with it every day.

Finally I reached the piano.

"Hello, Hans, do you still remember me?" I said, extending my hand.

Shocked, as if I were contagious, he took a step back.

"I don't shake hands," he said, "not with women."

He explained to me in detail why, as a pious Jew, he wasn't allowed to touch me. There was a gleam of triumph in his eyes. I knew that his indignation was a sham. Before me, at least twenty women had approached him with extended hand, and every time he had performed the same pantomime. He had recoiled from each of them and then bored them for some minutes while reciting sections from the Talmud and the Torah. I had no patience with it. While he was still talking to me, I resolutely turned my back on him.

In the kitchen I found Alex standing near a stack of boxes from a bakery. He was putting plastic cups on a tray. I gave him a kiss on his cheek.

"Have you been inside yet?" he said. "Have you spoken with the Great Guru yet?"

He laughed, but his expression was pained. For a moment I thought he was about to open his heart to me. Then he regained his self-control.

"Would you please help me with the pastry?" he asked. "Miriam went to the neighbors to borrow extra chairs. And I'm so clumsy today."

"Just tell me what I can do for you."

He pointed to a stack of plastic plates.

"There should be a ginger sweet roll on each plate."

I moved the pastry boxes from the overcrowded table to the kitchen counter, but there wasn't enough space there either. All the white plastic plates and forks went sailing through the air.

"Oh God," Alex said with a sigh. "There go the kosher plates." He looked at his watch. "It's too late to replace them," he said. "The stores are closed."

"Can't we just pick these up?" I suggested.

"Are you crazy? If Hans sees that, he'll kill us."

Helplessly we looked at the floor.

"Disposable dishes," said Alex. "The name is fitting."

For a moment we hesitated. Then, in common impulse, we both dove. In a panic, we grabbed at the plates. They were absolutely everywhere. We crawled around on all fours.

"Now for the forks!" I panted.

"Yes, the forks!" panted Alex.

At one point my forehead banged against his. Our eyes met. I saw the corners of his mouth tremble. We let ourselves fall backwards, plates and all, and laughed till we cried.

"What's with you?" shouted Thérèse.

We lay at her feet on the kitchen floor and gasped for breath.

"The forks," I cried out, tears rolling down my face.

"If Hans saw this," roared Alex.

The tears rolled down our cheeks.

When the audience had finally consumed the coffee and ginger sweet rolls and when everyone was seated, Stella Silverberg made her entrance. Because she, like me, seldom came to the synagogue, I knew her only superficially. She was a realtor and dressed with an eccentric elegance. That evening she wore a chic gray suit and a small black hat with a veil. She was followed closely by a gangly young man, unknown to me, in a leotard with panther spots and a purple sweater. His long hair was tied in a ponytail. Like a zombie he walked behind Stella, his eyes staring straight ahead, as though he didn't see anyone in the room. Miriam got up to introduce herself to him, but Stella shook her head and whispered, loud enough for everyone to hear: "He doesn't shake hands."

I nudged Thérèse who was sitting next to me.

"Could he be Orthodox, too?" I asked softly. "He certainly doesn't look it at all."

Deep in thought, Thérèse started. "What did you say?" she asked. "Who?"

"That boy in the spotted leotard."

"That's Stella's son," said Thérèse. "He's schizophrenic, not Orthodox. He's in treatment."

Meanwhile, standing in front of the piano, Hans was giving us a lecture. He spoke about the horrors of our time. Like a schoolmaster, he explained that war and famine, floods and other natural disasters, poverty and epidemics, all were the writing on the wall, the labor pains of the Messiah's birth. We had reached rock bottom. But the choice was ours. We could hasten the coming of Mashiach by leading a God-fearing and pure life.

I only half-listened to what he said. I kept looking at his lower jaw and the little grubby beard that grew there. With each frenzied movement of his mouth, the longest hairs of that little beard came in collision with the enormous Adam's apple jutting out of his thin neck. He didn't stand still for a moment. He skipped and tripped and swayed his head back and forth. I imagined myself back in my parents' house where my father, as if in a trance, danced through the living room while he addressed the Brothers of Gibeon. I broke out in a sweat.

"I'm getting sick," I whispered to Thérèse.

"Who isn't?" said Isidore, who was sitting behind us.

Hans had picked up a booklet from the piano and was waving it around.

"Then the eyes of the blind will see again and the ears of the deaf will hear again!" he shouted. "The lame will jump like the antelope and the tongue of the dumb shall sing songs of joy!"

I got up from my seat and squeezed between the rows on my way to the door. In the kitchen, I drank a glass of water.

"Are you all right?" said Isidore, who had followed me.

I nodded.

Kindly, he patted me on the shoulder.

"All evening I've been wondering what I would do if I had a son like that," he said, "but I'm still not sure. I can't decide between kicking him to death and slow strangulation."

The cantor of our congregation also came in. He had caught Isidore's last words and sighed. "Strangulation seems drastic. That boy just needs a girl. He needs a good screw."

Isidore brought his fingers to his lips in a silencing gesture. "Watch out, mister," he said. "If you use language like that, the Messiah will never come!"

During his visit to Holland, Hans announced his desire to

move to the Holy Land. In September he left for Israel, where he started his training for the rabbinate. Alex and Miriam boasted about his talents. Didn't they notice that a painful silence fell whenever they brought the conversation around to the subject of their son? Behind their backs, we wiped the floor with their darling boy.

"What a brat!" said Thérèse. "For a few years he's flipped through some books, and now he thinks he has a monopoly on wisdom."

"The way he stood there shouting," I said. "*Then the eyes of the blind will see again and the ears of the deaf will hear again!* It was just creepy."

"He was like Goebbels," said Isidore.

Rose, kind-hearted and gullible as always, felt that we were unnecessarily gloomy.

"Other boys his age get addicted to alcohol and drugs," she said. "They go out at night and rob old people in the streets. Be glad that Hans reads the Torah. A bad thing doesn't come from a good thing."

But she couldn't convince us. We were long past the stage of dismissing Hans's fanaticism as an innocent symptom of adolescence.

It was 1992. A year earlier, during the Gulf War, the Chabad movement in Israel had caused quite a stir. After Saddam Hussein threatened to bombard the country with Iraqi poison gas missiles, the Israelis barricaded themselves in their homes. Cracks and windows were sealed up with tape. Everyone, young and old, was given a gas mask. But while most of the population sat under the table, gas masks on, fearing for their lives, Chabadniks walked in the streets without masks. Their clairvoyant leader Schneerson had announced that these missiles wouldn't pose any danger. When events proved him right, the popularity of his movement increased. From Tel Aviv to Jerusalem, Chabad missionaries set out to work. In tanks and vans, they rode through the country to call people to prayer. Hans joined them.

Meanwhile he kept bombarding me with propaganda leaflets. In December I received another letter from him. In it he told me that he had gone on a pilgrimage to Hebron to pray at the cave of Machpela. In this cave, he wrote, Abraham and Sarah, Isaac and Rebecca, and Jacob and Leah were buried. Hebron was, according to Hans, the holiest place on Earth, the be-all and end-all. Where did Adam and Eve live after their expulsion from Paradise? In Hebron. Where did King David reside during the first seven years of his reign? In Hebron. And where, at the end of time, would the Messiah start his triumphal procession? In Hebron. It was outrageous that Palestinians had built a mosque on top of the cave of Machpela. Wasn't it written in black and white in Scripture that Abraham had bought the cavern as well as the ground around it for four hundred pieces of silver? Hebron was a

Jewish city. If the Palestinians did not want to recognize that, then they should just leave.

When I showed Thérèse the letter, she recognized the handwriting immediately.

"Do you save these?" she said. "I always tear mine up as soon as they arrive."

"Then you receive letters from Hans, too?"

"Absolutely. But if you've read one, you've read them all. The message is always the same, just like the Evangelical Network."

"Does he rail against the Palestinians in his letters to you?"

"How would I know? I throw them in the garbage can unopened," said Thérèse.

"In this letter he calls the Palestinians mangy dogs and liars. He writes that if they don't disappear from Hebron voluntarily, they'll have to be driven away by force. That's not a very gentle attitude for a future rabbi."

Thérèse sighed. "The Palestinians in Hebron haven't been exactly gentle to the Jews. In 1929 they killed practically every Jew in the city."

"But *all* Palestinians didn't participate in this?"

"No," she acknowledged, "but hate has a long life."

"That hate is part of recent times," I said. "In the Middle Ages Jews lived peacefully among Arabs. The caliphs were intelligent and tolerant hosts. And the Jews, in turn, were grateful guests. Not only did they make Arabic their spoken language, but they also wrote their books about geometry, astronomy, and medicine—to name a few—in Arabic."

"Still they were second-class citizens. They had to wear special clothing and pay high taxes."

"Yes, but no Arab stood in the way of their development. Under Arab rule they flowered; under Arab rule they felt at home."

"They weren't allowed to build synagogues."

"That's beside the point. They weren't persecuted. They were respected in science, literature, commerce. And they reached high positions at court."

Thérèse shrugged her shoulders.

"Palace Jews," she said. "You had those in the Christian world as well."

"In the Christian world, palace Jews were the exception that proved the rule. And the rule was that Jews were slaughtered by the Crusaders. The rule was that Jews were roasted over fires by the Cossacks. Their lives were in jeopardy. From one day to the next they could be banished or forced to live in stinking ghettos, because the king wanted to fill his treasury or because the queen was bothered by her corns."

Thérèse laughed, but I was serious.

"Medieval Arabs had more respect for Jews than twentieth-century Europeans did. Until recently the greatest Jewish thinkers were dragged through the mud. In Germany in 1933, an anti-Semitic book with photographs of Jews was published. Its title was *Juden sehen dich an*. Among others, there was a photo of Albert Einstein with the caption *Not yet hanged*."

"Even Freud was driven away," nodded Thérèse. "He couldn't stand the harassment. House searches by the Gestapo, Stormtroopers all over the place. But he had to ransom himself, and he wasn't allowed to leave Vienna until he had paid an enormous sum of money."

"In the Arab caliphate, insulting a Jewish scholar was unthinkable," I said. "They had a deep respect for knowledge, whether held by Muslims, Jews, or others."

Thérèse poured some hot chocolate. We were sitting by the potbellied stove in her studio while the rain beat against the windows.

"So you think that Jews and Arabs should reconcile," she said.

"I don't know whether we've ever been brothers, and I doubt that we'll ever become brothers. But if you accept the Torah literally, then the Arabs are the closest relatives we have, our first cousins. Shouldn't we draw conclusions from that?"

"You're forgetting," said Thérèse, "that many Jews in Israel are refugees from Morocco, Tunisia, Libya, Iraq, and Iran. They lived there for hundreds of years, but they were treated like animals by those tolerant Arabs of yours. And now they have to embrace these same Arabs? You can't expect the impossible."

"Is it really so impossible? You live among people who have worse things on their conscience than that. While half of them tried to murder you, the other half looked on indifferently. They dragged you to the other end of the world, where they raped your mother, gassed your father, threw your brothers and sisters into a pit, starved your aunts to death, and shot your uncles in the back of the head. There's no cruelty too appalling for them not to have committed. And you came back to these people. Every day you walk among them on the street, and you say good morning, please, and thank you to them."

"Yes, but you can't dwell on it. You lick your wounds, you straighten your back, and you go on with life."

"If that's possible," I said, "shouldn't it be much simpler to live in peace with the Palestinians?"

The longer Hans lived in Israel, the more militant his letters became. Finally he had a suitable target for his frustrations. His parents, at whom he had originally aimed his anger, had barely resisted him. In the Palestinians he found enemies of stature. Like a gift from Heaven, their existence legitimatized his rage, the rage of a toddler who wants to open the door but who is too small to reach the doorknob, and it gave this rage an adult air. Finally, the world would take him seriously. In his letters, which he now wrote on the computer, the better to send out more at once, he called the Palestinians sons of bitches and worms, syphilitics, murderers, and fascists.

* * *

One afternoon Miriam came to my door by bicycle. Her blond curls were windblown, and her forehead had frown lines that I'd never seen before.

"Do you have a minute?" she asked.

She lowered her eyes; she hadn't been in touch for months. Even in the synagogue she had avoided me.

I laughed.

"What is it?"

"Nothing. I suddenly remembered the first time that you rang my bell. You invited me for a Jewish evening."

She nodded. "And you asked what in the world you'd be doing there."

"You said that it would be very nice."

"But I hadn't even finished pouring coffee and passing the cookies when Rose and Isidore started in about concentration camps."

We roared with laughter.

"You had just moved," I said, "and boxes were piled everywhere. You were very pregnant, and a month later Hans was born."

Her face became somber.

"Hans," she sighed, "Hans."

While we were walking to the living room, she told me that he'd left for Hebron.

"To *stay* there," she emphasized. "He's left Jerusalem and is planning to abandon his education. We don't even know his new address, we have only a post-office box number. But he can't be living in a post-office box."

"What does he want to do in Hebron?"

"Pray, fast, wait. He says the Messiah is coming."

"How does he figure that?"

"He's calculated it."

"Then I hope he's better at counting than at spelling. The letters he sends me are full of mistakes."

"He's not a language genius," admitted Miriam. "But he does have a vast knowledge of Jewish issues."

"In that case he should know that it isn't kosher to predict when the Messiah is coming. The Talmud expressly advises against it."

Miriam shrugged her shoulders.

"The greatest Talmudists have made predictions," she said. "Rashi, Nachmanides, and so on."

"That only proves that even the greatest Talmudists have done stupid things."

"According to Hans, the Messiah should be landing shortly, in the cave of Machpela."

"Landing? Is he coming by spaceship?"

"It is written that he will descend."

"So much is written. It says that he will descend, and it says that he will rise from among us. It says that God will send him when the time is ripe, and it says that God will hasten his coming. It says that redemption will come when we have bettered our lives, and it says that that won't happen until we have sunk to the deepest possible depravity. And there's much more that can't be reconciled. In the Talmud all these contradictions are cleverly balanced so that no one can complain afterwards that he was fooled."

"So you think that all this is fraud?"

"The stories about the Messiah are so ambiguous and so enigmatic that they make it quite possible for us to deceive *ourselves*. Has redemption not yet come because we live in sin? Or are we not sinful enough? It's a mystery to me."

"Hans says that many messiahs have been born and have died. They were ready to redeem the world, but the world wasn't ready for them."

"Hans says, Hans says," I repeated impatiently. "It is indeed asserted that a Messiah lives in every generation. But somewhere else it says that the Messiah is an exceptional individual who will overshadow all preceding prophets, someone who will surpass Solomon in wisdom and be greater than Moses."

Offended, Miriam averted her eyes. When she looked at me again, there was mistrust in her glance.

""Do you actually believe in the Messiah?" she asked.

"I don't know what to believe."

"Do you long for his coming?"

"He'll appear sooner or later, but I'm not looking forward to it."

"What do you mean?"

"I'm afraid that we can't expect much good from Hans's Messiah. He's a tyrant of the worst kind. Anyone he doesn't like immediately, he hurls into the sea of fire. Anyone who doesn't cheerfully beat his machine gun into a plowshare gets the death penalty. Even Stalin didn't finish off his victims that thoroughly. Once in a while he would send someone to Siberia to cut down trees."

"What do you expect?" said Miriam. "You can't redeem the world if you don't eradicate evil."

"Has the thought ever occurred to you," I said, "that the world *cannot* be saved? If people could stop bashing in each other's brains, why haven't they done so? Nothing is preventing them from making a promising start today, or perhaps tomorrow, when they come home from work."

"They can do it, but not without help. That's exactly why they need the Messiah."

"Nonsense," I said. "The Christians have had their Messiah for almost two thousand years, and it hasn't gotten them anywhere."

Miriam looked put out.

"If you don't believe in the coming of the Messiah, then you place yourself outside Judaism," she said. "If you don't long for his coming, then you basically reject the whole Torah. That's what Hans says."

"Fortunately I don't depend on Hans for my salvation," I said angrily.

"What do you mean?"

"Yesterday he didn't know the difference between Genesis and a hole in the ground, but today he considers himself the greatest scriptural scholar of all time. And you go along with that. You even invite your best friends to let themselves be threatened by him with Hell and damnation."

"Do you mean the lecture he gave? You're the only one who was upset by it."

"Everyone was upset by it; everyone thinks that Hans is a conceited pain in the ass who's in urgent need of a spanking. But I'm one of the few who will say so."

"Alex and I also don't agree with all his opinions," said Miriam stiffly, "but we're impressed with his perseverance and his enthusiasm. In the past he would run after a soccer ball all day long. His interest for Judaism has given direction to his life."

"That's wonderful," I said, "but it's no reason for him to force others to change their lives in that direction. That goes for you, too. I don't like being cross-examined by you!"

"Cross-examined?"

"Do I believe in the coming of the Messiah? Do I secretly doubt the salvation of humanity? Am I a good Jew? Who should decide that? You, who make Judaism into a theatrical performance? Don't make me laugh."

Miriam stood up.

"My God, what a bitch!" she said, putting on her coat. "I

knew it all along, but Alex kept insisting that I was imagining it. You never did anything for the Jewish community. You watched while we worked like mad to get people together, to find a rabbi and a cantor, to organize prayer services. You never lifted a finger. No wonder you hate Hans. He embodies everything that you're not. He doesn't avoid responsibility—he puts himself at the service of others. He lives totally in the spirit of the Torah."

She stalked out of the room, but I followed her.

"He sends letters in which he calls Palestinians worms and syphilitics," I said to her back. "He'd prefer to run them out of Israel today. Is that in the spirit of the Torah? If only he'd stayed on the soccer field, where he'd do considerably less harm."

Miriam trembled with rage. "At least he dares to believe in something," she said. "And he makes no secret of it. Yes, he's sure of what he's doing. But should you reproach him for his conviction just because you yourself doubt everything?"

She was already outside and was angrily fiddling with her bicycle lock.

"Do you know why the Talmud says that we're not permitted to make predictions about the coming of the Messiah?" I said, standing in the doorway. "Because if he doesn't come when we expect him, we might despair. And desperate people are capable of the most awful things."

She didn't react. Judging me unworthy of another glance,

she got on her bicycle and rode off, disappearing around the corner.

During the following months I was quite busy. In May, the *Northern Daily* moved to a new building on the outskirts of Groningen. And when I had finally found my niche there, I was transferred from the national and foreign affairs editorial staff to the city desk. Soon I discovered that I knew far too little about municipal politics in general and about those of Groningen in particular. The city turned out to be a world unto itself, with its own balance of power and its own conflicts of interest. Before I'd done mainly work in the office, but now I was almost constantly on the move. At the city desk there was no day or night shift; all the journalists were on duty from early morning until late at night. In my spare time I studied old transcripts of municipal council meetings and other files in order to make up for my lack of factual information. I hardly had time for anything but work.

Hans kept sending me letters and flyers, but following Thérèse's example I now threw each envelope with its cramped writing into the wastebasket unopened. I did this without qualm. But I found it much more difficult to ignore his parents. Since our quarrel Miriam hadn't called me. Nor did I do anything to break the icy silence. Because I didn't know what else to do, I stopped going to gatherings of the Jewish community. I even avoided the company of Rose, Isidore, and Thérèse.

Meanwhile I felt guiltier all the time. Why had I felt compelled to tell Miriam the truth? Why had I put our friendship on the line? Wasn't friendship more important than any truth?

One evening in August I got a call from my mother. I recognized her voice, but the connection was bad. There was an ominous whistling in the phone, as if she were standing on the polar ice cap in a snowstorm that was about to blow her away.

"The Eternal has given and the Eternal has taken away," I heard her say. "The name of the Eternal be praised."

Was she doing missionary work among the polar bears?

"Is it you, *Mameh?*"

"You don't need to shout so," she said, "I hear you fine."

"Yes, but I can barely understand you."

"Your father is dead. His heart stopped. It happened while he was saying his morning prayer. He suddenly fell forward to the floor and he stopped moving."

What did she mean, *he stopped moving?* I saw my father before me again, the way he became entranced during the meetings of the Brothers of Gibeon. The way he shook and danced, swept away by the sound of his own voice. He hadn't stood still for a moment, but had he ever really budged? With his petrified thoughts he had been as unyielding as a pillar of salt.

I tried my very best to feel something, but I didn't succeed. My mother was calm, too. She gave the impression that she didn't have to control any sorrow.

"He died as he lived," she said matter-of-factly. "In the hands of the Almighty."

She was right; he had been a tool in the hands of his supposed Creator. As long as I'd known him, he had blindly obeyed strict laws. Day in and day out, he'd sat bent over Scripture without the slightest feeling for the characters who were portrayed in it and without the least understanding for the flaws that they displayed. Even the greatest heroes of Jewish history had deviated from the right path, even the staunchest patriarchs and the bravest kings had known moments of weakness. Cunning and deception, murder and carnage, love and lust: nothing human was foreign to them because they were involved in life. My father, in his pride, had placed himself above them and outside the world. Yes, he had been virtuous. But how useful was the virtue of someone who had never exposed himself to any temptation whatsoever?

I promised that I'd come to the funeral, although I was obligated to no one—especially not to the deceased himself, who had declared me dead years ago and who had never wavered from that decision.

The next day at the crack of dawn I left for Putte, near the border of Belgium. There, south of Bergen-op-Zoom, religious Jews have been buried for generations, not out of preference but because they can't get a suitable resting place in their own country. Jewish law prescribes that the dead remain untouched until the Messiah raises them from the dust on Judgment Day. But that's too long for the Belgians, who refuse to contribute their fine soil for that. According to Belgian law, a grave must be cleared by the end of one hundred years. This is why Jews who won't let wild horses kick them out of Belgium while they're still alive nonetheless are forced to emigrate after death. My father was such a posthumous emigrant.

When I arrived at the cemetery, it was black with hats and white with beards. About five hundred people had gathered to pay their last respects to my father. The period of mourning for the destruction of the Temple had just passed. Those present, who for days had listened to the traditional lamentations in a dimly lit synagogue, were quietly waiting for the ceremony to start. With unwilling steps I proceeded into the crowd. It took a while before I found my mother. She was much older and grayer than I remembered.

"I no longer recognize you," I said in Yiddish.

"In twenty years quite a few wrinkles have been added," she answered stiffly.

Like total strangers we faced each other.

"Did *Tateh* ever talk about me?"

I asked it in a muffled voice, almost whispering.

"Der Tateh?" She looked at me searchingly. "About you?"

"He must have said something; he must have mentioned my name at least once?"

I searched her face for a hint of pity. But her eyes remained cold as ice.

"Why would he?"

"Maybe he missed me."

"If that was the case, he never let on."

"Never at all?"

"You can't blame him. You have only yourself to thank for all this."

"He sprinkled ashes on his head, he cast me out."

"You could have written a letter. You could have done so many things; you could have talked with him."

"Talk, with him? It was impossible to talk with him."

"You haven't changed," she said bitterly. "You think only about yourself. Did you come here to drag your father through the mud? Go right ahead. He can't defend himself now."

At that moment, the president of the funeral society began the prayer.

He, the Rock, His work is perfect. He is just and fair. Is He not your Father who created you? Did He not make you and give you your destiny?

The crowd began to sway back and forth and murmur. In its motion, my mother was pushed forward to where the coffin with my father in it was lifted mysteriously, as though floating. Then the procession started moving.

I walked at the rear, blinded by tears, while from hundreds of mouths resounded the old psalm: *His angels will protect you, wherever you go. They will carry you on their hands, so that your foot will not stumble on a rock.* Over and over the casket was set down reverentially, and over and over new bearers pushed forward to lift it. When they finally lowered their burden into the earth, I turned around. The path seemed made of foam rubber. With the unsteady steps of a moon traveler, I left the mourners further and further behind until even their many-voiced prayers were out of hearing.

On the way back to Groningen I cried in anger. Apparently my father had succeeded in banishing me not only from his house but also from his thoughts. Me, the daughter on whom, for lack of a son, he had pinned his hopes, the daughter whom he had educated as though she had been born to be a rabbi. For years I had been subjected to his rigid discipline. While other girls of my age still played with dolls, I had had to learn Hebrew and read the Torah under his watchful eye. But when I finally took my destiny into my own hands, he crossed out my name from the Book of Life. And since that time I'd never been completely sure of my existence.

Angrily, I pushed down on the gas pedal. Through the windshield I looked up at the sun. Could it possibly revolve around the Earth anyway, without anyone noticing, just because my father had willed it?

I had a headache by the time I got home. I closed the curtains and fell into a short but deep sleep on the sofa in the living room. I awoke in the early evening. The pain had retreated to behind my eyes, but the throbbing increased every time I thought of the funeral and of my mother's brusqueness. To distract myself, I turned on the television.

A documentary about the black rhinoceros in Zimbabwe was on. A biologist was reporting that the animal was still being hunted for its horn, which, when ground to powder, was supposed to increase male potency. Druggists, quacks, and shamans sold the stuff for exorbitant prices. To prevent the last remaining eighteen rhinos from being sacrificed to this superstition, conservationists had decided to remove their horns. From a small airplane the animals were shot with a dose of anesthesia. Then someone used a Black and Decker saw to remove the horn just above the root. The shrill sound of the saw cut through me like a knife, and I turned my eyes away. When I looked again, one of the animals had regained consciousness. Drowsily he was scrambling to his feet. His horn lay next to him on the ground. On his head a dark stump remained. On both sides of it his small eyes blinked in surprise at a hornless horizon.

I quickly switched to another channel. There the news was in full swing. Excited men with hats and sidecurls were moving on the screen. For a moment I expected to see my father's coffin. But this wasn't Putte, this was Israel.

In the streets of Hebron fierce clashes broke out today between Jewish settlers and Palestinians. One of the settlers suddenly started shooting. A sixteen-year-old Palestinian was hit by three bullets and died on the way to the hospital. The perpetrator, a twenty-one-year-old Jew, originally from Holland, was overpowered by Israeli soldiers. He said that he had been acting according to orders from God…

That was Hans, without a doubt! For a few seconds his face filled the screen. Around his mouth hovered the same triumphant smile I saw when he refused to shake my hand in his parents' house.

Hebron on the occupied West Bank of the Jordan River has for years been the scene of battles between Palestinian and Jewish extremists. The cause of the continually flaring hostilities is the cave of Machpela where, according to tradition, Abraham, forefather of the Jews as well as the Muslims, is buried. Both groups consider this place the cradle of their culture and demand possession of the grave for themselves.

Several residents of the small Jewish quarter of Hebron spoke. Behind them rose the dramatic barbed-wire barricade that they had built to fence themselves off from the outside world. They declared that no Jew in Hebron was safe from the hatred of the Palestinians. Some called the murder a sad but unavoidable chance occurrence. Others openly declared their approval or admiration for Hans's act. According to them he had given the Palestinians what they deserved, an eye for an eye, a tooth for a tooth. One of them pulled a pistol from his pants pocket under the fringes of his prayer shirt and waved it angrily in front of the camera. "You don't think that we can go out into the street unarmed, do you?" he shouted stridently. "This is the jungle, sir! We have been thrown into the lion's den, like Daniel. We are here among wild animals!"

I got up and walked around the house like a sleepwalker, from the living room to the kitchen and back again. As I went, I did meaningless things as if in a trance: I took a magazine from the table and put it back again in the same place, I opened a drawer and pushed it shut again. My headache was forgotten; I was now overcome by a feeling of acute panic that numbed all of my senses.

After a while I dialed Thérèse's telephone number, but no one answered.

I had better luck with Isidore and Rose.

"Yes," Isidore said with a sigh, "we've also seen it."

"Maybe it wasn't Hans," I said. "Maybe it was just someone who looked exactly like him."

"No, it definitely was Hans. Thérèse has already spoken to Alex and Miriam on the phone. We're going over there. Rose and I were just about to leave."

"Do you think that I could go there, too?" I said hesitatingly.

"That all depends," Isidore said sharply. "If you feel compelled to say that Hans should have stayed on the soccer field, then please don't come. Alex and Miriam can figure that out by themselves. They don't need you for that."

Apparently Miriam had told him all about our confrontation.

"It's easy to laugh at others' mistakes," he said. "After the camp Rose could no longer have children. We've always thought that was terrible. But secretly I sometimes think that we should be glad about it. I don't know what I would have done if Hans were *my* son. Would I have had a terrible fight with him? Would I have kicked him out of the house? And would that have helped? I'm in the fortunate position of not having had to make that decision."

"Do you think Miriam would like to see me?" I asked.

"I don't know," said Isidore. "It wouldn't surprise me if she didn't feel like it on an evening like this. But that isn't the point, is it? The question is whether you think it's worth giving it a try."

"I'd like to try," I said.

"Then we'll meet you there," said Isidore, "in fifteen minutes."

In the car I was hot with shame. Isidore was right. What did we know about having children and enduring lifelong worries about them? I remember years ago, when Hans was still a toddler, how Miriam had told me that she couldn't sleep at night because she was afraid that something would happen to him. With eyes wide open and ears alert, she lay in the dark ready to jump up at the slightest sound and attack any danger whatsoever. She wasn't afraid even of the devil.

Had my mother in the distant past watched over me as passionately? Perhaps, perhaps. But not after my eighteenth birthday. Then, because my father had cast me out and because the book of Leviticus justified it, I no longer played a role in her life.

Miriam and Alex, on the other hand, had continued to love their son against their better judgment. The further he had distanced himself from them, the closer they had locked him in their hearts. The more peculiarly he started behaving, the more fiercely they defended him to others. They had braved their own doubts and the ridicule of half the world. For that you needed courage, the kind of courage that my parents had lacked.

Thérèse opened the door after I rang the bell. She gave me a quick kiss, as though we'd seen each other only the day before. Nervously I followed her to the enclosed porch where Alex, Miriam, Isidore, and Rose were sitting.

"What you need," I heard Isidore say, "is the advice of a specialist. Not just any lawyer, but a very good one."

"We'll find one," said Alex. "But we didn't hear until five o'clock this afternoon. We haven't been able to do much yet."

No one looked surprised when I came in. Isidore pushed up a chair and I was automatically, almost casually, included in the conversation.

"Do you think that they know yet at the paper?" Alex asked me.

"I didn't go to work today," I said, "but I can find out tomorrow."

"If there's anything I'm not in the mood for," said Miriam, "it's having journalists all over the house."

She placed her hand on mine for a minute.

"Except for you, of course," she said.

Alex started to cry. The tears streamed down his cheeks and he did nothing to stop them. It was as if he didn't even notice. He sat at the table, motionless, while his face kept getting wetter.

"We should never have let him go to Hebron," Miriam said softly. "All the lunatics from Israel are concentrated there. Of course they used him. It's not like Hans to walk around with a pistol, let alone shoot it. When he was small I once took him along to the veterinarian. Yupi's claws needed to be cut, but that man cut too close and one started bleeding. Hans began to sob terribly. He never could stand to see blood."

"That was the blood of a parrot," said Alex somberly. "He seems to have less difficulty with the blood of Palestinians."

"Perhaps that boy provoked him. You don't know," said Miriam.

"But how?" said Alex. "He didn't have a weapon; they emptied his pockets and found nothing, not even a knife."

"You don't know," repeated Miriam.

"We *do* know," shouted Alex. "Hans confessed. And a whole crowd of witnesses was standing right there."

"It's hard to believe," mumbled Miriam. "The day before yesterday he called and asked if I would buy socks for him. 'The socks here are of such bad quality,' he said, 'after a week they've got holes.' "

"And he's even proud of it!" said Alex, covering his eyes with his hands. "He seems to have said that he wants to clear the way for the Messiah. And I can believe it. For months we've been getting the craziest letters from him."

"Yes," said Miriam. "He had dreams in which Isaiah and Jeremiah appeared to him."

"They gave him messages and orders," said Alex. "He had to erase the name of Amalech from under the heavens. That sort of thing. He felt called to action; he felt like a hero."

Miriam nodded.

"He was totally confused. I even sent him a small bottle of valerian drops."

"It all started with Antwerp," said Alex. "I should never have let him leave the local school. But I was busy. I had just started that new project and was working sixteen hours a day. Hans was the least of my worries. The very least."

Isidore tried to console him.

"You're not responsible," he said.

"Don't say that!" said Alex. "I'm his father. If I'm not responsible, then who is?"

"Even Hans isn't responsible," said Isidore. "Someone who thinks that he gets orders from Isaiah and Jeremiah, someone like that can't be held accountable. He needs to see a psychiatrist."

After this a deep silence fell, during which Thérèse got up to pour coffee.

When, a moment later, she pulled shortbread out of her bag, Isidore started laughing.

"Women!" he said. "A disaster happens and what do they do? They think of *shortbread*."

"A disaster with shortbread is easier to bear than a disaster without," contended Thérèse while cutting the shortbread into pieces.

"That reminds me of when I was young," said Rose. "Whenever disturbances against the Jews broke out in our village, my mother brought the most delicious things out from the cellar. Then we would sit, the shutters closed, and eat the whole supply of canned fruit, as if it were a holiday. 'Hurry up,' my mother would say, 'or do you want the anti-Semites to take it with them?' Because during those disturbances, Jewish homes would be completely ransacked."

"All right then, let's do it," Miriam said with a sigh as she was handed a wedge of shortbread. "I haven't had a bite to eat yet."

"Please give me two pieces," said Alex. "I can't bear the thought of leaving even a crumb for the anti-Semites."

* * *

Hans was charged with murder. He was sentenced to three years in prison and two years of compulsory psychiatric treatment. Alex and Miriam visit him in Jerusalem as often as they can manage.

Not long ago Hans sent me a letter from prison. *The end is coming*, he wrote, *the end over the four corners of the land. The day is near. Blow the trumpet and be ready.*

With some regularity I give his parents packages to take along to him. They contain chewing gum and socks, and, if it works out, the newest *Suske and Wiske* comic book.

I've offered my translation of the poems of Samuel Ha-Nagid to several literary magazines, but there's no interest in them. Meanwhile I'm translating the poetry of Moses Ibn Ezra. He too was a Jew who lived in medieval Spain. He too fought on the Islamic side against the Christian monarchs. Twice he witnessed the destruction of Granada, and twice his heart was broken.

It doesn't seem likely that my translations will ever appear in print. But that doesn't matter very much. Through them I'm able to fulfill the holiest of all Jewish commandments, the commandment to keep on learning.

BETTE

Give her of the fruit of her hands;
and let her own works praise her in the gates.
—Proverbs 31:31

E VER SINCE SHE LEARNED THE NAME OF HER ILLNESS, she's barricaded herself behind books. The books are always changing, but each one serves the same purpose. Each book is upright as a shield in her hands. Each book protects her eyes like a visor. Reading seems incidental. She does read, but out of stubbornness. She reads in order to trick death.

"I'm not paying any attention to you," say her eyes that follow the lines, "I've got more important things to think about."

If her legs could still hold her, she'd walk menacingly through the apartment, from room to room, and arrogantly slam the doors. But her legs have let her down. They rest uselessly on the small bench in front of her chair. She did try to throw them into the battle.

"Look here," she called out to the Angel of Death. "Are these the legs of an old lady? These are the legs of a girl. Go away, you've come years too soon."

And the Angel, who seldom gets to see such legs, whistled between his teeth. But he didn't leave. Each morning, when she awakens, he is the first to bend over her. In the sunlight that shines through the ocher curtains, his oval face seems made of gold. It shines at her like a mirror.

"I used to feel so happy when the sun shone in the morning," she says with a sigh.

Now she dives fearfully back into the half-light under the sheets, and she calls for me.

I'm her daughter and I come immediately. Initially I had offered to sleep next to her, in the place where my father used to sleep just two years ago. But that's where the books are stacked up from one end to the other. Books by Anton Chekhov and Mary Renault, books by Isaac Singer and Barbara Tuchman, by Graham Greene and Iris Murdoch, by George Orwell, Natalia Ginzburg, Marguerite Yourcenar, and many others.

"These books," she says, "have to stay there. You can't take them away."

They look like the ramparts of a fortress, a hastily constructed fortress that threatens to collapse at any moment. From time to time I straighten the stacks and push them against each other, but minutes later they tilt again to the edge.

"It's good that your father can't see this," she says. "Whenever he would start a new book, he'd open it in the middle first and then, very carefully, section after section, the rest. That way the spine wouldn't break."

Because the books lie there, I sleep in the room across from hers. We keep the doors open so that I can hear her. In the middle of the night she starts to moan. I'm instantly awake. I jump out of bed and go to her.

"Come, come," I say, "be still."

I press my lips to the small hollow of her right temple that is turned toward me.

"My head hurts so much," she sobs. "It's the tumor. I dreamed that a hole opened in the middle of my face, a hole as big as a fist. And you were all standing around my bed and you looked inside, through that hole. And everyone was disgusted by it."

"By you?" I say. "How can that be? How could we be disgusted by you? It was just a dream. You're sweet."

I pull her to me. She lies gasping in my arms. To sit like this, with Bette against my chest and the Angel of Death against my back...The reading lamp shines in my eyes. I rock her a little, I hum, I talk.

"If we could just go to the beach together," I say. "Do you remember that time when we put two chairs in the waves? The water splashed around our ears."

"Yes," she says, "yes."

But she doesn't really listen. She doesn't care what I say, as long as I keep talking. I could just as well rattle off the Pythagorean theorem, or the capitals of the United States, or the first poem I had to learn by heart in school, "The Staff of Johan van Oldenbarneveldt," by Vondel:

> May my wish protect you unsullied,
> oh staff and support, that supported no traitor
> but freedom's champion and Holland's father
> on that cruel scaffold.

I remember that at the time, as a ten-year-old girl, I didn't understand the poem at all and went to Bette for an explanation. She was in the kitchen draining boiled potatoes.

"May my wish protect you un*what*?" she shouted, her head enveloped by steam.

"Unsullied."

She looked at me sideways and burst out laughing.

From that time on, as I was leaving for school in the morning, she would give me a kiss and straighten the collar of my coat, then jokingly say: "May my wish protect you unsullied."

Has she ever taken me seriously? Does she take me seriously now? Does it still matter, or do I no longer care?

She notices my discomfort.

"Am I too heavy?" she says softly.

"Not at all," I assure her. She isn't heavy. In the past few months she has wasted away to the bone. Yet she hangs on my neck like a leaden weight.

To sit like this, with Bette as unidentified dying object in my arms. There is no manual for it. *Seven ways to console your moaning mother, at night, dressed in your pajamas.* No one ever told me how it should be done. And there isn't enough time to learn now.

During the day, the garden brings respite. She reads at the open window, I walk barefoot through the grass. Looking over her book, she gives me hints and orders.

"That mint is worse than weeds," she calls out. "And you might thin out the sage. What are those teasels doing there?"

"Where?"

"Over there, near the bitter rockcress." She points. "I don't like teasels."

Among the snowy white rockcress, enormous teasels are indeed raising their dark heads.

"Well, they like you," I say.

But the teasels find no favor in her eyes.

The more control she loses over her body, the closer the watch she keeps over the garden. Anything that grows rampant must be restrained. I run around with shears and a trowel. Standing on a wobbly stepladder, I prune the elderberry bush. With a kitchen knife I remove thistles and dandelions from the lawn. I release the ivy from the embrace of unruly bindweed. Sometimes crouching, then kneeling, I move along beds of delphinium, yarrow, impatiens.

CARL FRIEDMAN

This garden is the work of her hands. She planned it around my father, when he was still alive. She planted hedges and shrubs to protect him, to keep him safe, this man who had come from afar, this man who had felt the whip and had seen the smoke of the ovens. Henceforth he would be spared all disaster, he must never more be harmed by anyone or anything. She had decided this. In the remote corner of the garden where he liked to retreat grew blue-plumed veronica called honor-and-praise, violet hearts-ease, as well as an exotic plant called burning love, on stems at least a meter high, with scarlet red clusters. Whatever evil the garden couldn't ward off, Bette herself drove away. On her girlish legs, she would dance light as a feather around my father's chair, stand behind him, press her cheek against his cheek, and say: "Who would have thought it then? That you would give me three children. That I would have you with me for so many years." Then his gaze would become dreamy. She was the only one who could make him forget his despair, even if only for a moment.

She would never have let him die, as I did in my ineptitude. He had already been ill for months when it happened. We had taken care of him together. He could no longer stand or walk, and he had stopped eating. He lay in a bed on wheels in the living room. Day and night we changed him and his sheets, his sheets and him. We read no newspapers, we heard no news. The world could have perished while we danced our ritual dance around his bed. Time stood still, as though eternity had already begun, and we hurried about foolishly with tubs of bathwater, dirty linens, clean pajamas. Bette especially became exhausted. The night of his death she had fallen into a deep sleep. I tried everything to wake her: I pulled her up by her shoulders and shook her, I called and begged, but her head rolled back on the pillows like a rock.

Without Bette to cast her spell, my father was lost. Without Bette to protect him, evil could find him. Like an icy-cold wind that cannot be shifted by hedges or bushes, the evil of many years poured over him in these last hours. All the gas chambers blew open and a procession of ghosts streamed around his bed whispering. He braced himself, struck out with his fists, clutched his sheets. But it was all useless; the gas had caught up with him.

It wasn't until then, at my father's deathbed, that I saw in their full dimension the horrors that, with Bette's help, he had tried to master all his life. But I may not speak about his last night. Bette has forbidden it. In the gray light of dawn, after she had tried in vain to revive him, she silenced me.

"He died peacefully in his sleep," she said in a tone that permitted no contradiction.

She replaced the torn sheet with another. She tried to straighten his fingers, but they remained clenched in a fist. She tried to close his eyes, but they remained half opened. The left eye was glazed. The translucent right eye looked down from the corner, desperate and full of disgust, as if next to his bed yawned a murderous pit.

This didn't escape my brothers' notice when they showed up later. Defeated, they stood by their father's body.

"Bergen-Belsen," said Wolf in a flat voice.

"Auschwitz," whispered David.

But Bette continued to insist that he had gone to sleep. And Bette is always right.

I crawl along the flowerbeds while Bette is framed in the bedroom window. When I look at her, she quickly lifts her book.

"What are you reading?" I call out.

She shrugs her shoulders and mumbles something.

I saunter over to the window.

She complains of pain. She has, she says, been sitting up too long. With difficulty she struggles up out of the chair. She doesn't wait for my help. She pulls herself up on the windowsill and stumbles to her side of the wide bed.

"Can I do something for you?" I ask when she is lying down.

"The grape," she says gruffly, "has to be tied up."

"The grape?"

"Against the garden wall. The new runners are destroying the roses."

"I didn't know you had grapes."

"But you ate them last year."

"Purple grapes?"

"No, white ones. You don't even remember."

"It seems so long ago."

She doesn't answer. Behind a wall of books she turns away from me testily.

The trip from Amsterdam to the Belgian village is long. From my front door to Bette's it is almost four hours. If I go back and forth in one day, I'm traveling for eight hours, more time than it takes to fly to New York. Half of that time I spend on the train, but then I transfer to a bus that takes me through the border area, mainly over bumpy roads, from hamlet to hamlet. That bus is mostly empty. The same passengers always huddle together on the front seats. They are patients from a mental hospital located halfway along the route. They all sit there, snickering at no one in particular, except for one. That is Andrieske, a dwarflike idiot of about fifty. He takes up a position next to the driver and screams at him continuously in the local dialect. Andrieske has a voice of tin, which I keep hearing hours later, when I'm at Bette's.

There's something oppressive about the landscape. During the Second World War my father fled from his pursuers through this area. Not by the road, but through the woods next to it. On every bus ride I see him running, far away, under the trees. His shirt flaps out of his pants, branches hit him in the face, but he doesn't slow down for a moment. Limber, he jumps across ditches. Like a spear, he shoots between the trunks. Once in a while he glances sideways, at the bus and at my silhouette behind the window. "Faster, Papa, faster," I say, "so they won't catch you." Where the woods end, he stops, but as soon as we pass through the next village, he turns up again, running between the trees.

"I've seen him again," I say, when I greet Bette.

"Your father?" she asks.

I nod. "He went faster than the speed of light."

She closes her eyes and leans her head back into the pillows.

"He really is an incredible man," she says blissfully.

Since February we have known that she is fatally ill. But it wasn't until May, when she could no longer get out of bed, that we were forced to acknowledge that something had to be done. David had a serious talk with her and then telephoned me.

"I asked her where she wants to die. In the hospital or in her own bed."

Silence.

"Yes?" I say. For David is a man of few words. He divulges only a minimum of information even when encouraged to tell all.

"At first she didn't want to give an answer."

Silence.

"Yes?"

"But I told her that the choice was up to her."

"And?"

"She prefers to stay where she is."

"That goes without saying," I said. "Back to the hospital—the idea is repulsive."

"I promised Papa."

"What did you promise Papa?"

"When he was dying."

Silence.

"Yes?"

"I promised then that I would take care of her."

"Oh, I didn't know about that. I mean I didn't know that Papa and you talked about these things."

"I promised."

"Of course."

"And if necessary, I'll do it by myself. But it will be easier if you'd help."

"I'll help."

"That's settled then," he said.

It sounded too simple.

"David?" My voice trembled. "I'm so afraid something will go wrong. It's a kind of stage fright, but much worse. As if you're sent on to the stage without having learned your lines. I mean, you can't practice for it. And if it fails, you never get the chance to do it again."

"Just be glad that it's a one-time performance," said David.

I wanted to say something in reply, but not a word passed my lips. I clapped my hand over my mouth and started to cry without a sound.

"You had the fright of your life," he said, "when you sat with Papa that last night. I don't know what happened that night, and I don't want to know either. But this time it'll be different, I promise you that."

"Do you think we'll manage?"

"You and I?" he said calmly. "I don't doubt it for a moment."

Wolf's name wasn't mentioned. That wasn't necessary. We were convinced he would do what he felt to be his responsibility. And Wolf's responsibilities always have business objectives. He works as a crisis manager. When a company gets into a crisis, Wolf comes in to restore order. His solutions are radical. The staff is downsized and half the employees are fired. Reorganization by liquidation. Wolf has no time for his mother. He's not surprised by one death sentence more or less, not even hers.

In February I talked with him once by telephone, when Bette's tumor had just been discovered. I appealed to his vanity.

"You're her oldest son," I said, flattering him. "It's you she needs more than anyone else. She wants to cry on your shoulder and she wants to be consoled by you."

I praised his insight and his life experience. I said that as a crisis manager he was the obvious person to take on the chaos within our family.

He asked me to keep it short. He was, so he said, about to leave for a business dinner.

Then I resorted to less diplomatic means. I sketched Bette's condition as it was at the time.

"She no longer eats anything, she's not approachable. When we come into the hospital, she just sits there, staring ahead indifferently. The announcement that she has only half a year to live hit her like a sledgehammer."

"Frankly," he said impatiently, "I don't understand why she's making such a fuss. Isn't there such a thing as euthanasia?"

From that moment on I banished Wolf from my thoughts.

Our crisis is kept under control by David. He does this without force, with the calmness that is his even in the most trying circumstances. Taking care of Bette is a labor-intensive activity, a five-day work week for him. He confers with the doctors, manages the financial affairs, handles the correspondence, does the shopping, and picks up medicines. He also keeps friends and family informed about the latest developments.

Starting in May, he hired nurses for morning and evening. The intervening time we divide between us. Because I have to travel such a distance, I sometimes end up camping in the village for days. In all, there are eight nurses who work in shifts.

I know each of their routines, I know their good qualities and their weaknesses, I know the names of their husbands and their children, and if they don't have children, then I know the names of their cats.

David calls me every evening.

"Can you still keep going?" he says. "The day after tomorrow I'll relieve you."

In between he often drives to the village as well. In her schoolgirl handwriting, Bette composes a shopping list for him. When he returns with full boxes and bags, she always finds a reason to criticize him.

"Salted butter," she says, disapproving. "How could you? Can't you read? I don't need anyone to salt my butter. If I want salted butter, I'll salt it myself. But I don't like salted butter, I can't stand the thought of it."

Without a word of protest, David leaves the house to exchange the butter. Sometimes she sends him back to the store as many as three times.

"Pre-cut onions!" she shouts indignantly. "They're for people who have no knives and no taste. Maybe your wife goes in for that, but in this house everything is cut fresh. And what sort of green beans are those? They look like cucumbers. Where did you eat when you were young? At my table you never had anything like that."

As soon as David leaves, she picks her book up again and starts leafing through it angrily.

"If there's anything I can't stand," she calls after him, "it's pre-cut onions."

When David isn't there, she lets me run around for her. One afternoon, after I've spent several hours picking currants at her urgent insistence, she repeatedly rings the bell next to her bed.

"Please go quickly to the shoe store for me," she says.

I wipe the sweat off my face. "In an hour or so," I say. "Right now I'm making jam."

"Can't that wait a bit?"

"No," I say, "everything is ready. The jars have been rinsed with soda and the pan with berries is already on the stove. You did want jam?"

"Yes, but not this minute."

"But I did get that impression." It sounds sharper than it was meant.

"Can I help it that you get all sorts of ideas?" she says. "While you were in the garden, I called the shoe store. They are such nice people! Because I can't go myself, they'll let you pick up shoes for me. They've put aside part of their summer collection so that I can choose from several styles."

"How many boxes is that?"

"I have no idea. About ten or twenty."

"How do I drag them all home on the bicycle? Can't David do it tomorrow? With the car it's much easier."

"I promised these people you'd come right away."

CARL FRIEDMAN

"Can't you call them back to tell them that I'll be an hour later?"

She shakes her head resolutely.

"No, I won't think of it. They're already doing much more than usual by letting you take them."

"What kind of shoes do you want?" I say. "You're barely able to walk. And even if you could walk, your feet are too wide, the veins are totally inflamed."

"I'll just take them three sizes larger. And if they still don't fit, then we'll make cuts in the sides."

"But you can't get out of your bed anymore. When do you want to wear shoes?"

"Why, when, how?" she says with a sigh. "Should I know everything beforehand? It doesn't matter. I'll ask someone else. There are plenty of people who are eager to do me a favor."

"I'll be glad to bike to the shoe store for you," I say, " but after I've put the jam in the jars."

"No, don't bother," she says stubbornly. "You've spoiled the fun for me."

The nurses say that David and I should interpret Bette's hostility as a compliment. "Your mother doesn't dare snap at others; to others she has to be friendly and grateful. Only with you can she give in to her frustrations. She knows you'll continue to love her no matter what."

This doesn't sound too unlikely, but is it true? I thought I loved Bette, I assumed it as a matter of convenience. But now, with her death so close, I'm not certain of anything anymore. Do I love Bette enough? Enough to endure her anger, her fear, and her despair for the duration of her illness? Death is a stern judge. He asks us questions that we never bothered to answer. He tolerates no ambiguity. He accepts no *maybe* or *probably,* he knows only the scythe.

When I'm in Amsterdam, she calls me frequently.

"Hello, dear, it's me. Did you know that in the Second World War the Americans wanted to launch bats against Japan?"

"Bats?"

"Yes, that's what I'm reading. Bats were trained to carry firebombs, which they were supposed to throw down on Japanese buildings. It was a secret operation. But during an experiment some bats escaped. Then bombs fell on an American army barracks and on a general's car, and then they stopped it."

"Interesting," I say.

"Disgusting!" she says. "If people want to kill each other, that's their business. But they should leave animals out of it."

Indignantly she gives a summary of animals that have historically been used for purposes of war: horses, donkeys, oxen, dogs, carrier pigeons.

"And what about the elephants Hannibal used to cross the Alps?"

"Yes," she says, "that Hannibal wasn't such a fine fellow."

There's always something urgent she has to tell me. That there will be a television documentary about the sex life of the kangaroo or about child labor in Pakistani carpet-knotting workshops. That I have to turn the radio on immediately because they're singing such beautiful songs by Fauré. And since we're speaking anyway, don't I agree that Yeltsin has an unusually untrustworthy face?

"What does Yeltsin have to do with Fauré?" I want to know.

"Nothing. I'm simply wondering how a man with such a face could have made it to the presidency," she says.

In the past she used to call me, but not more than once a day. Since she's become ill, she knows no limit.

"Everything okay, dear? I'm reading an article about the pyramids of Giza. Did you know that they drilled small holes in the north wall of pyramids? Through them the pharaoh would look outside, at the stars."

"Why did he want to look in that direction especially?" I ask. "Why not toward the south instead?"

"He looks toward the north because there's a star that always stays in one place."

"The Pole Star?"

"No, probably the star Thuban in Draco. For the ancient Egyptians that had the same function that the North Star has for us."

She heaves a deep sigh.

"When the dead person turned his gaze to the stars, it was easier for his soul to ascend to Heaven. There, in the heavens, lay immortality."

One evening, just as I arrive from a trip full of difficulties, and even before I've had a chance to put down my small suitcase, she starts a quarrel with me.

"You're almost two hours late," she says.

I explain that my train was delayed. "A suicide," I tell her. "Just past Utrecht a man had jumped onto the tracks from a railroad bridge."

"Did he have to choose rush hour for that?" she says, aggrieved. "A little consideration for others no longer matters."

"All trains on that section were rerouted," I say. "That's why I missed my connection. And to top it off, I saw the bus to the village pull away right in front of me."

"You should have called," she says. "One of the neighbors would have picked you up in a car."

"It was getting close to dinnertime. I don't like to disturb the neighbors then. If you'd been alone, yes. But I knew that a nurse was with you."

"The neighbors don't mind driving at all, they do it with pleasure."

"Now they do," I say, "but I don't want to wear out their kindness too soon."

"What do you mean?"

"God only knows how long you'll be ill."

"Are you losing patience?"

"Not me, but they might lose theirs. I don't bother others unless it's urgent."

"And do *I* do that?"

"I didn't say that. But if you really want to know, yes, I think that you take people's time rather lightly. I heard that yesterday you ordered the director of the bank to come to your bedside."

"I didn't order him. I asked him nicely to come, and he came willingly."

"He probably didn't dare refuse. These so-called requests of yours often sound like commands."

"What else could I do? I had no more cash."

"If you had just waited for David, he would have gone to the bank for you. By the way, what were you thinking of doing with all that money in bed?"

"You never know what will happen."

"What can happen, for God's sake?"

"They could be standing at the door suddenly."

"Who could be standing at the door?"

She shrugs her shoulders.

"Like that," she says morosely, "all sorts of people. Collectors for a good cause."

"Perhaps for building a retirement home for overworked bank directors."

"That man didn't mind it at all. He was happy to get away from his desk."

"Nonsense. Errand boys want to make it to director. But I'd like to see the director who enjoys playing errand boy. You let half the world slave for you. The hairdresser has to rush over to do your hair on her Sunday off. You call the bookseller out of his bed."

"I wanted to order a book."

"For that you don't have to wait until midnight."

"It was only eleven o'clock. How should I know that that man goes to bed so early? Without me he would have been broke a long time ago. I'm his only steady customer in this backward village."

She rummages through the books and papers on my father's half of the bed.

"Here," she says, "it was in the paper yesterday in a bold headline: *Seventy percent of Flemings never read a book.*"

"And to punish them for this you make their lives miserable."

"Please, shut up," she says scornfully. "You're the last one who should tell me what to do. As though you've got things together so brilliantly! You claim you don't need anyone, but is that something to be proud of? No wonder all men run away from you screaming."

"Only one man has run away from me, and he did that at my request." I pick my small suitcase up again. "Do you think that I've come all the way from Amsterdam just to be insulted by you?" I say. "Look for someone else to take your abuse. I'm leaving."

"It's too late to go," she says. "You won't get home tonight."

"Then I'll spend the night in a hotel."

I walk away, but she jumps up. With very small steps and holding onto the walls, like a drunken bird, she hops after me.

"Don't go," she moans. "Please, dear, I beg you, stay here."

I walk to the living room. My throat is tight with distress.

Out of breath, she stops and hangs onto the door handle. She almost falls forward, but I drop my suitcase and just manage to catch her in my arms.

The nurse too comes running out of the kitchen. "Does it have to be like this?" she says, reproving. Together we drag Bette back to her bedroom. "Are you staying?" she asks.

I nod. "Yes, I'm staying," I say softly.

When Bette is back in bed, I go outside. In the furthest corner of the garden I start sobbing desperately.

"Are you all right?"

The nurse has come after me and puts an arm around my shoulder. Reassuring me, she explains that all terminally ill patients go through this phase.

"Your mother is furious at the fact that she has to die. She simply can't believe it, she refuses to accept it. But that will change."

Suddenly there appears before me the vision of another

Bette, a calm one, whose resistance has been broken. She no longer opens any books. She speaks to us graciously. Drowsily, she leans into the pillows, completely reconciled to her fate, and asks me whether she could perhaps, if it isn't too much to ask, have a cup of tea. It's a Bette who would be a thousand times more objectionable to me than the fighting, furious one. Is the nurse right? I bend my head and sob harder. I feel as if I'm looking into a deep abyss.

O God, I pray, don't humiliate her. Keep her anger for us. Let her be as bitter as gall, let her rattle her chains, let her wrestle with the Angel. Until the moment of her death let her remain under the illusion that the outcome of the fight has not been decided.

Friction arises even between David and me. I envy his calm and equilibrium. I envy the equanimity with which he endures Bette's outbursts, simply turns away from her and then, with a glass of beer in hand, goes to sit on the terrace in the sun. He chats with the nurse on call; he gives me a friendly nod. When I complain about Bette, he shrugs his shoulders without a word.

"Oh well," he says impassively.

Where did he get that patience of a saint?

"For you it's simple," I snap at him. "You don't have to stay here for days. You come, you chat, you drink a beer, and you leave again. After each visit to this house, you can go back to your own world. But I sit here imprisoned. I'm slowly going crazy here."

"If this drives you crazy," says David, "then you should come less often and stay for a shorter time."

"That's impossible," I shout. "Without me, you would be saddled with everything."

He smiles. "That's not your problem, is it?"

"Of course it's my problem."

"You don't seem to think much of me," he says with a vehemence that surprises me. "A chat and a beer. Do you really think that's why I drive all the way out here? Do you really think that I don't have any difficulty with all this? What do you actually know about me? Do you know whether I'll sit and cry in my car later? What do you know about the depth of my despair?"

On getting up he knocks over his glass. He picks it up with a shaking hand. Then he walks toward the house.

"David!"

Frightened, I run after him. In the kitchen we stand face to face, with the table between us.

"David, I'm so sorry. I admire you especially because of what you do and how you do it. I wish I were as calm as you. I wish I had more patience with Mama."

Bent slightly forward, his hands on the edge of the table, he looks at me seriously.

I'm reminded of the morning after my father's death. Since

none of us had eaten, David offered to get rolls, and I went with him. We walked silently side by side down the long village street. Halfway to our destination, it started to snow. Small, thin flakes blew into our faces.

"Papa didn't die peacefully in his sleep at all!" I said suddenly.

I waited for him to ask something, but he remained silent.

In my anger I began walking faster. He barely kept up with me.

"Don't you care what happened to him?" I shouted.

He ran after me.

"Anyone can see what happened to him," he said.

He grabbed my arm, but I shook him off.

"All right then," he sighed. "What happened?"

"He was gassed," I said.

On David's face a sad grimace appeared.

"You think that I'm crazy," I said.

"Not at all. You haven't slept for nights, you're simply exhausted."

We kept on walking side by side. The snow thickened and became heavier. I thought of my father's grave, of the men who were digging it in the frozen ground. We crossed the village square, but David suddenly stopped. He pulled me toward him and took me in his arms. There we stood, on that large square, in an awkward embrace.

Now, two years later with equal discomfort, we stand miles apart.

"I love you," I say.

Although I mean it, it sounds false.

"It's all right," he answers.

I would like to embrace him as before, on the way to the baker. But I can't move, my legs seem paralyzed. And he doesn't move either.

"Should I still pick up the medicines?" he asks evenly.

"Yes," I say, "the pharmacy closes early today."

"Then I'd better go," he says.

But we are still leaning on the table, each on his own side, deep in thought, too tired to leave our positions.

There are still moments of affection, although they don't last long. Bette's tumor demands all of our attention. It races ahead of us, and we sprint after it, David and I, in turn. We hardly have time for each other; our meetings are brief. We're like relay runners who relieve one another. There's a nurse in the house all afternoon now. But our tasks don't lessen; instead, they increase.

Once, on the train going south I pass a meadow full of cows. It's afternoon. Most have sought out the shade of a large oak tree at the edge of a ditch, but two cows stand apart. Flank to flank, in the full sun, they lick a flat stone in the grass. Their enormous pale tongues move simultaneously and touch.

When I reach the village, I find David sitting in the garden, reading the paper.

"How are things?" I say.

"She's asleep. The doctor has been here three times."

"Three times?"

"Yes," he says in a muffled voice. "Don't be afraid."

Silence.

"What shouldn't I fear?"

"There's a lump on her face."

"A lump?"

He avoids my eyes.

"What kind of lump?"

"A very large one."

Silence.

He points to his jaw. "Here," he says, "around her mouth."

"When did that happen?"

"Last night."

"And what does the doctor say?"

"That it's part of the clinical picture."

"That it's part of the clinical picture? As if we couldn't think of that ourselves. Healthy people don't have lumps."

"She wants to have radiation."

"Again?"

"This time just where the lump is."

"My God," I whisper.

He nods.

"Again that dragging back and forth to the hospital," I say. "She simply can't keep it up. And what's the sense?"

"It's not up to you to decide whether it makes sense or not," says David pointedly. "It's *her* lump and she can do with it what she wants."

He's absolutely right.

Silently we sit on the terrace, in the scorching heat of the summer that is Bette's last. Around us a swarm of crickets is chirping. I bend my head and cry. David strokes my hair.

Sobbing, I tell him about the meadow that I saw from the train.

"Are you crying because of *that*?" David says, surprised.

"No, I'm crying because soon Bette and I will never again lick the same stone."

"Oh, sweetheart," we hear.

It's Bette's voice.

"Come to me quickly," she calls.

I run through the kitchen and the hall to her room. She's sitting up in the pillows and stretches out her arms. Books fall from the bed. We lie flank to flank.

"If only I were a cow," she says later, after we've dried our tears. "I look like the Elephant Man."

The lower half of her face looks as if a vicious stranger's clenched fists were rising just under her skin.

Because the heat continues, the garden demands much attention. Evening primroses, cattails, maiden pinks, carmine berries—everything is in bloom. Even the touch-me-nots have opened.

Buzzing monotonously, bees fly in and out of the calyxes.

"Please stop for a bit," says David.

I've just treated the roses for aphids, and I'm weeding again.

"*Il faut cultiver son jardin*," I say.

He lowers his voice. "What good will this do? Soon there will be new people living here. They'll probably turn all this under."

With a finger on my lips I walk up to him.

"I do it for Bette," I whisper. "As long as I think it's worthwhile to work in the garden, she won't die. At any rate, she's under that illusion."

"Oh, come on," he says, "she knows quite well that she has at most a month left."

"She knows it," I nod, "but she keeps hoping for a miracle. She's fooling herself. And I help her with that."

David looks at my dusty hands.

"So it's all for show?" he says.

"Of course."

"But then you don't have to work so hard, do you? From her bed she certainly can't see those weeds."

I wipe the sweat from my eyes.

"You're right, she doesn't see them," I admit. "And yet I do my work carefully, because I've come to believe it myself."

"Believe what?"

"That with a rake and a hoe I can keep death away."

* * *

Keeping death away. I devote hours to it every day. Maybe I can chase away the Angel who is still waiting at the edge of the bed. Under no circumstance must I let on that his presence oppresses me. I water the lawn and the plants. I remove wilted leaves and spent flowers. But I also do things that are expressly directed toward the future. For example I prune last year's berry bush canes so that they'll bear more fruit next year. Finally I tie the loose grapevines, training them to climb up against the garden wall.

"What are you doing?" calls Bette, who hears me hammering.

"I'm tying up the grapes," I tell her later, at her bedside.

"You don't need a hammer for that, do you?"

"Oh yes, because the trellis has rotted underneath and has to be replaced. Don't you want to eat grapes again next year?"

In the hospital, molds have been made for a mask that she has to wear during the radiation treatment. It looks like a death mask and fits tightly over her face. Where the tumor is, there is a hole. When I see her for the first time with that mask on, my uncertainty is gone. I love her. How could I ever have doubted that?

She not only looks like John Hurt in *The Elephant Man*, but now she also talks like him.

As soon as the nurses put on the mask, an animal fear overpowers her.

"I'm suffocating," she squeaks, "I'm suffocating."

At every treatment she asks: "That lump can't burst, can it? I once dreamed that."

The nurses try to reassure her, but the specter keeps haunting her.

"I dreamed that there was a wound so deep that you could look through it and see inside me. Everyone was disgusted. And you know," she says softly, "I *don't* want them to be disgusted by me."

Afterwards she comes home exhausted. She sleeps until the evening meal.

At night she leans against my chest. Two fans are humming, but the air remains tepid and heavy. Neighbors are having a garden party. From the dark comes loud music, which doesn't bother us, doesn't concern us.

"I still had so many plans," says Bette.

"What had you wanted to do?"

"All sorts of things," she muses. "Make a balloon trip. Take piano lessons. Buy a telescope. None of that will happen now."

Bette is devoted to the stars. She owns a star catalogue, and every year the Astronomy Society sends her an astronomical calendar. In it are data about the positions of the planets, their conjunctions with the moon, their paths around the sun, their shortest distance to Earth and thus to Bette herself. Each calendar contains surveys, tables, and celestial maps on which the brightest stars are shown.

As easily as her friends chat about Dior and Chanel perfume or about recipes for apple pie, Bette speaks about the moon in ascending and descending node or about the central meridian of Jupiter. Before her illness she recorded her personal experiences with the heavens in a thin gray-marbled logbook. Regularly, when the weather was clear, she would sit in the park behind the house, gazing up, using my father's binoculars. She never got around to buying a telescope. She was too modest for that. We all acted somewhat silly about her nighttime escapades, my father especially, since he hated to wake up in a half-empty bed in the middle of the night. Why couldn't his wife just stay in bed instead of roaming around all by herself through the park, and on such legs? God knows what unsavory characters might be leering at her through the bushes, while she had eyes only for the elongation of Mercury. For quite some time he gallantly accompanied her, but he didn't share her passion for the heavens. More often he sat next to her fidgeting or paced around her bench sighing impatiently. Finally he left her to her fate; she would have to deal with the consequences.

"We could give her a telescope," I say to David one day. It's almost Bette's birthday, the eighth day of the eighth month.

"What use will she have for it?" he says.

"Of course she'll use it, even if she looks through it for only five minutes."

"How do you propose to do that? Can you see us dragging her around in the dead of night? And she can't sit on a bench anymore."

"I've figured it all out," I say. "We bring her to the park in a wheelchair, and a bed will be ready for her there."

He squeezes his eyes almost shut.

"A bed," he says. "Hm."

"An already made bed," I say, "so that she can look at her ease. August is a good time, the sky will be alive with meteors."

"I was actually planning to give her roses," he says, still hesitating.

"We'll give her roses, too. Seventy roses at breakfast."

"Well, all right then, let's do it," says David.

A few days later we drive together to an optical instruments store in Antwerp. The selection of telescopes is greater than we thought. There are telescopes for beginners and for the advanced, with or without mirrors, with a moon filter or a polar alignment, hand-operated or computer-driven.

We choose an instrument that magnifies the sky seventy-two times.

"Is that enough?" I ask.

"With this scope," says the man in the store, "you can see even a speck of dirt in God's eye."

* * *

On a Sunday afternoon, unexpectedly, Wolf comes walking up the garden path. He carries a baby in his arms and has two toddlers hanging on his pants legs. They are the children from his third marriage. The son from his second marriage, a skinny adolescent with pimples, shows up a moment later, dribbling a ball.

Wolf's behavior is charming.

"He can afford to be charming," I say softly to David. "He is, so to speak, *paying a visit*. What does he know about our problems? He's only a spectator."

But David will hear nothing of that.

"Everyone does what he can," he says. "That's true for you and me, and it's also true for Wolf."

When Wolf has drunk two cups of coffee, he begins to yawn.

"Poor boy," says Bette, "are you that tired?"

Wolf sighs and rubs his face. "I've worked so hard this week, I can hardly keep my eyes open."

"Then go and lie down for a while," she says.

He takes off his shoes and walks out of the room in his socks. In the open doorway he turns around. He presses his hands against his chest.

"Lately I've had these stabbing pains," he says. "Here, right near my heart. Maybe I should have a cardiogram done."

When Wolf has retreated to the living room, Bette also feels tired. David and I take the children to the park.

"Finally he manages to come by," I hiss to David, "and he takes a nap!"

But David shrugs his shoulders.

"Isn't Bette pleased?" he says. "What's good enough for Bette is good enough for me."

The radiation is finished. Bette has been treated seven times, her mouth is burned inside and out, but the tumor won't go away. He is resolved to stay and extends his territory visibly. Red with victory and gloating with malicious delight, he continues his campaign. Inch by inch, he advances inside her face. He exults because there is a surprising amount to be destroyed along the way. To hell with that chin! Pound against those sweet lips! Her nose can be even more crooked, still thicker! Use the whip, and again!

Fortunately she still has her hair. Black and abundant, it falls around her deformed head lying in the pillows. She now eats only pap: pap made with flour and pap made with grains, pap with rice or with rusks. Patiently she lets herself be fed by me. Groggy with fever and morphine, she closes her eyes more and more frequently. But when I want to take away the book that she's holding, her fingers close around it like a clamp.

"No, dear," she mumbles sluggishly.

Her voice comes from far away, she is almost asleep.

"You must never put away my book," she says with a thick tongue.

"I'm sorry, I thought you were asleep."

"I can't sleep without a book," she says. "My eyes may be closed, but the words blow in."

"That saves you a lot of trouble," I say, and I press the book still closer into her grasp.

A smile appears around her crooked mouth. Her eyes cloud over again.

She becomes nervous about her birthday.

"Will I still make it?" she keeps asking us. As though dying at seventy is to be vastly preferred over dying at sixty-nine.

We're just as tense as she is. From a nearby home for the aged, David has obtained a high bed on wheels that will be delivered in the afternoon. At first they didn't take him seriously. A bed that has to be delivered to a park? For a deathly ill person who is going to lie in it and look at the stars at night?

We gaze anxiously at the sky, and we read the weather forecasts.

"If only there isn't a thunderstorm," says David. "The heat's already lasted so long."

On the morning of her birthday, the sky remains cloudless. Bette insists on receiving her guests in the living room. For days she has worried about the clothes that she'll wear. That blue silk blouse? No, the blue makes her face look even more pale. The apricot-colored jacket? No, that accentuates the red-ness of the swelling. The first decision must be the right one, since dressing twice is too exhausting.

The white dress into which she finally lets me help her isn't flattering either. Her arms, thin as insect legs, stick out of the three-quarter-length sleeves.

"The Bride of Frankenstein," she mutters when she sees herself in the mirror I hold up for her.

"Not to worry," I say while I brush her hair. "You still look better than many other women your age."

I name a few of the women who are going to come and visit in a while.

Bette sighs.

"I'd still like to trade places with them!"

"Because they're going to outlive you?"

She nods.

"Would you like to be Martha?"

"Even Martha."

Martha, the upstairs neighbor, looks like a hippopotamus. She's blond and blubbery. I've never been able to figure out where her double chins end and her bosom begins.

"You don't mean that. You would never want to go through life as Martha."

"If that were the price for turning eighty?" says Bette. "I'd do it in a minute."

"Retroactively?" I ask. "Because to be Martha at eighty, you also had to be Martha at sixteen. Imagine that. No boy wants anything to do with you. You're too fat for dancing."

"Then I'll just sit and read."

"What are you going to read?"

"What did I read when I was sixteen? Louis Couperus, Hermann Hesse."

"Martha reads only cookbooks and embroidery patterns."

"That's not fair," says Bette. "I'd be bored to death."

"Well," I say, "either you're Martha or you aren't."

Because of the blisters on her mouth, Bette can't put on lipstick. She does powder the tumor at length. But a little while later, just as mold appears on a damp wall, the tumor darkens again on her face.

She's worked herself up for nothing. The guests barely pay attention to her. She seems to become thinner and more silent, while the company speaks passionately of matters of vital importance.

"How do you like that new diet of yours?"

"Just fantastic, I can eat everything except carbohydrates. In the morning my breakfast is an ounce of cheese and a cup of yogurt. At noon I eat lean roast beef with pickles. And in the evening I eat steak with an enormous salad."

"How can you lose weight that way?"

"I don't know, but it works. I even eat mayonnaise. And I can also have white wine."

During the entire visit, Bette holds herself up bravely in her chair. But as soon as the last guest has left, she starts crying from exhaustion. We bring her back to bed. She seems to have a high fever.

"It's been too much," says the nurse. "Now she'll need days to recover."

In the afternoon the bed is delivered to the park. We place it not too far from the path, with the foot toward the pond. I make it up to look festive, although it's doubtful whether Bette's fever will go down before the night.

David mounts the telescope on the wooden tripod and adjusts the height. He extends the legs, lies down on the bed to look through the lens, jumps to the ground, and tinkers some more.

Toward evening we receive a call from Wolf, who had gone the day before with his family for a vacation near Bordeaux.

"The weather is gorgeous!" he exclaims. "Tomorrow we're going to take a glider above the Dordogne."

He wants to congratulate his mother, but her fever is too high for her to accept his birthday wishes. She is shivering and delirious.

"She won't die, will she?" I whisper to David. "She can't do that—she has to look through the telescope first."

He heaves a somber sigh. "See the stars and then die."

"What should we do about the bed?"

"I'll throw a plastic sheet over it," he says. "We won't lose heart."

Not until four days later does the fever subside.

"If I were you," says the nurse, "I'd forget the whole business. She's not really aware."

But I pull the plastic from the rented bed, David takes the telescope out of the shed, and we both hope for the best. Around midnight we bring Bette outside. Nodding off from moment to moment, she sits in her wheelchair. She is barely aware of what is happening. Like an object, she lets herself be moved around by us. We don't have to go far, the park borders directly on the garden. But as soon as David places her on the bed, she falls into a deep sleep.

Dazed, we stand in the grass. Around us, the village is quiet. The crickets chirp rhythmically, and occasionally a duck quacks. But we listen to Bette's heavy breathing, which repeatedly stops and then, rasping, begins again. How small she is under the open sky. It is now that we truly see how little of her body the illness has spared.

"She'll wake up soon," says David.

"She still has to take some pills," I say.

Our voices have a hollow sound, as hollow as the tin voice of Andrieske in the bus that goes to the mental hospital.

"She won't sleep forever," David adds.

But tonight appearances are conspicuously against him. It's

as though her death starts here. It's as though this narrow bed will take off at any moment, to set out for the zenith, with nothing but stars before its bow.

At half past one she calls out my name. David and I, who have both lain down in the grass, jump up simultaneously.

Her hand gropes in the air.

"Turn on the lamp, please," she mumbles. "I can't find the switch."

"You're in the park," we explain. "You're getting a telescope for your birthday."

"Oh yes, it's my birthday," she says. "Have the visitors left yet?"

"The visitors have left. And we've come outside to look at the stars."

"*Isti mirantur stella*," she mutters.

She almost dozes off again, but we give her a drink of water. I push the pillows far under her shoulder blades. David adjusts the telescope to focus the image. The metal barely touches her cheek; she is jolted wide-awake.

"Is this the hospital?" she asks. "Are they going to give me radiation?"

Panicked, she touches her face.

"Shouldn't I have my mask on?"

"No," says David, "this is the park. The only radiation here is from the stars."

He has finally maneuvered the lens in such a way that Bette can see the sky.

"The Perseids," she sighs. "It's a whole swarm."

Meteors flash in the eastern sky. Like magic, one after the other, they shoot like rockets from their places.

"Cassiopeia, Andromeda."

She's talking to herself.

"There is Cetus," she says. "And that must be Mira. I've never seen it so clearly."

"And Leo?" asks David. "Where is Leo?"

Bette was born under that sign.

He first moves the tube up and then to the right.

"Leo is gone," says Bette. "He's in the other hemisphere."

"Couldn't he have waited?" says David.

"Who?" she asks sleepily.

"Leo."

"Is he waiting? I don't know any Leo."

Her eyelids close again.

"Tell him that I can't come. All my shoes are too small. It's so late, I'm tired."

Before she has a chance to fall asleep, David lifts her into the wheelchair.

"No, no."

She starts crying plaintively.

"It's much too late, I don't want to. I don't have my mask on."

"Shush, you don't have to," says David. "You don't have to go anywhere. I'm taking you home."

He pushes the wheelchair quickly over the grass.

"No," Bette begs, "please."

She sags forward and sobs: "I'm so tired, so tired!"

At two o'clock everything is back to normal. Bette is lying in her own bed. David and I sit in the kitchen.

"I forgot her pills," I say. "Should I wake her again?"

He shakes his head.

"Let her sleep, for God's sake."

"She still has to take them tonight."

"I know, but not right now."

The door to the garden stands open. A moth flutters against the lamp. David stands up and restlessly paces through the kitchen. He sticks his hands in his pockets and takes them out. He walks back and forth, and he sighs.

"Why are you still sitting here?" he grumbles suddenly. "Why don't you go to bed?"

"Will you give her the pills later?" I ask.

"Goddammit," he says. "Goddammit."

He flings his arms around his midriff. His face is ashen, he bites his lips.

"What's the matter?" I say. "Do you have a stomachache?"

But he doesn't have a stomachache, he's crying.

I can't remember ever having seen David cry, not even

when we were small. His tears are of another order than mine; mine come and go like the tides. His sorrow is immense and disconsolate. Should I say something to him? I wouldn't know what. Nothing more can be done. Bette will die, that's now certain. Strangers will live in this house. The village will become a name on the map. I look up at the moth that is tottering over the lamp with spread wings. If only it were all past: David's sobbing, the fight with the Angel, the waiting for Godot.

Dog-tired, I reach Amsterdam for a breather of three days. Here, where I have all the time to myself, I should be able to relax. But as soon as I dare to sit down, I'm assailed by emotions that I had suppressed in the rush back there. The panic that I didn't allow myself to feel, the rage that I swallowed, the despair that grew quietly, they're all catching up with me. It's true, in the village I have no peace. But in Amsterdam I have no life. Aimlessly I walk from room to room. How is Bette today? And will David water the lawn the way I urged him to do?

"David, you're not forgetting the lawn, are you?"

"Do you have to call me for that? I didn't forget."

"And are you remembering the plants on the terrace?"

"I spray them, too."

"No, don't spray, the flowers will get wet and then they'll be scorched by the sun. You should water only the soil."

"Fine, I water the soil."

"How is Bette?"

"She's asleep. We really are managing without you. Why don't you go and do something nice?"

"I wouldn't know what to do."

"A movie?" says David. "A concert? Change the channel and think of something else."

I stand at the window and look at the bustle down below. What am I supposed to do on the street? I would rather weed for a few hours, weed blindly in Bette's garden.

At night I can't sleep. I lie on my back and listen. Is Bette awake now? And when she moans, does David take her in his arms? Does he sing songs for her and read to her, as I do? David doesn't like singing; even in kindergarten he hated it. And he seldom reads books. He doesn't know the passages that Bette likes to hear and that calm her. Does she even dare to cry in David's presence? I wonder, I really wonder.

In the morning I decide to paint my apartment. I clear the walls of the living room, I cover the furniture with a tarp, and I rent a scaffold. In the tropical summer heat I paint the high, sculptured ceiling. While doing this, I don't have to think about anything. The only resistance that I encounter is easy to overcome: as long as I keep moving my hand, the paint automatically yields to the brush. Carefree, in a T-shirt and shorts, I'm standing on my scaffold. I have changed the channel.

When the time comes to travel back to the village, I don't have the courage. I buy more paint and start on the walls. I keep postponing my departure. Downstairs, in the depths, the telephone rings. There are voices on the answering machine, but they don't concern me. It's only David's voice that can make me descend reluctantly.

"Should I no longer count on you?" he says impatiently.

"Oh yes, no, I don't know."

"You don't know?"

"No."

"That doesn't help me. You haven't been here for ten days."

"I'm painting the walls."

"May I put you on the schedule or not?"

"That depends," I say while scratching dried-up paint from my upper arm.

"On what?"

"So much still has to be done. I've bought a new couch that's being delivered tomorrow. I'm also getting new curtains and cherrywood bookcases."

"I don't care about your bookcases and your walls. Are you coming or not?"

"Maybe next week."

"What a situation," he says, exasperated. "My mother is near death, my brother is on vacation, and my sister has gone crazy."

I scratch paint from my legs.

"Are you still there?" he shouts. "I don't understand this at all."

"I simply can't come," I say. "The water is much too deep."

"What water? What are you talking about?"

"*There were two royal children, who loved each other so much.*"

"Oh, *that* water."

"I would like to go to Bette, but I can't get on the train anymore, I can't take the bus anymore."

"As long as you won't regret it."

"The water," I say, "is too deep."

A week later he checks in again.

"David here. I'm calling from a telephone booth," he shouts.

"What are you saying? From where?"

"I don't know; around the corner from you."

"In Amsterdam?"

"I hope so. If this is Brussels, then my car has a serious defect."

"I suppose you want to visit me?" I ask.

"That was the idea."

"It's a mess here," I say.

"Are you still painting?"

"No, I'm changing everything. The bed is going into my study, my desk is going into the living room, and from now on I'll eat in the kitchen. That way I'll have an extra room."

"And what will you use it for?"

"I'll have to think about that."

"Then you won't have time to come and have a cup of coffee with me somewhere?"

"If it doesn't take too long," I say.

But we aren't going to have coffee at all. As soon as I sit down next to him in the car, David drives in the direction of the freeway.

"Are you taking me to Bette?" I ask when we leave the city.

He nods. "It's high time. Any longer and you won't be able to carry on a conversation with her."

"Is she deteriorating that fast?"

"According to the nurses, the tumor has reached her brain. Once in a while, when she gets tired, she talks nonsense. She still makes shopping lists, but I can't make any sense of them."

He rummages in the glove compartment.

"Just look," he says, handing me a small sheet of paper that appears to be covered with writing. But on closer inspection each word is a line of scallops with a loop here and there. This is what preschoolers do when they pretend to be writing. I look at it, horrified. Are these innocent scribbles made by a woman who more than fifty years after finishing school could still translate Homer and Virgil almost effortlessly? My eyes fill with tears.

But David extends his hand and points.

In the midst of the scrawls, in clear letters, my name appears at least twice.

"I just had to get you," he says with a wink. "You're the only errand on the list that I could decipher."

Not until much later, when we've almost reached the village, he says: "She wants to give you her jewelry today."

"Bette? To me? But I never wear jewelry."

"I know that. And she knows it, too."

He looks at me out of the corner of his eye.

"She's been talking about it all week," he says emphatically. "For her, this is something solemn. A way of saying goodbye. A goodbye to her daughter."

I heave an unhappy sigh. What kind of daughter am I anyway? While Bette was scrawling my name on her shopping list, I was standing on my scaffold not thinking of her at all.

She has become even thinner. With a shawl around her shoulders, she sits in bed.

"Hello, dear," she says when I enter.

"Hello, Mama, here I am again."

I look for a place on her face where I can plant my lips, but the tumor is everywhere.

Desperately, she clutches me to her.

"I thought I'd lost you," she whispers. "I couldn't reach you anymore, the connection was broken."

It's the beginning of September. The great heat has

passed, the windows are closed. Downhearted, I look outside. The garden looks neglected. The flowers in their beds are mostly withered. The grass is the color of hay. There are deep cracks in the ground, as though in my absence an earthquake has occurred.

"We've waited so long for you," says Bette.

She speaks slowly.

"The garden," she says, "and I."

From behind the books she lifts a box, which she places on her lap.

"Come here, near me," she says, while taking off the lid. "I want to give you my jewelry. Soon it may be too late."

Stiffly, I sit on the edge of the bed.

"Each piece of jewelry has its own story," she says, and she begins to tell them, one at a time. There are bracelets and rings, smooth stones and cameos. Sometimes she holds a necklace against the light, and next she displays earrings on the palm of her hand.

When she has given each piece of jewelry a story and instructions for use, she takes off her wedding ring.

"It was my mother's," she recounts slowly.

While speaking she gasps for air. I have to make an effort to understand her.

"Her name and that of your grandpa are engraved on it. At the time, your father and I had no money for a ring. It was only a year after the war, and he had tuberculosis. But the date on the ring is correct, because we got married on the same date as they did."

"On purpose?" I ask.

She nods.

"It's not a beautiful ring. So coarse and old-fashioned. I could have had it changed, but I've never wanted that. It's practically the only thing that I have of my parents. I've forgotten their faces a long time ago. I don't even remember their voices."

"Why don't you keep on wearing it yourself?"

"No, you should have it," says Bette, determined. "It's ugly, but no one says you have to wear it. You only have to keep it."

When I have put the jewelry away, her eyes close.

"Would you read something for me?" she asks. "I'm so afraid to sleep. It helps when I hear voices."

She presses a book into my hands.

"I had started the Song of Songs. But it's impossible. I can't read anymore; I see only half of what's there."

I sit down on the chair next to her bed and I read. My speaking sounds almost like singing.

> *I was asleep but my heart stayed awake.*
> *Listen!*
> *My lover knocking:*
> *"Open, my sister, my friend,*

my dove, my perfect one!"
I opened to my love
but he had slipped away.
I sought him everywhere
but could not find him.
I called his name
but he did not answer.
Swear to me, daughters of Jerusalem!
If you find him now
you must tell him
I am in the fever of love.

To sit like this and read to Bette. Her head droops forward. Once in a while a crooked smile breaks through the tumor.

How is your lover different
from any other, O beautiful woman?
My beloved...towers
above ten thousand.
His eyes like doves
by the rivers
of milk and plenty.
His mouth is sweet wine, he is all delight.
This is my beloved
and this is my friend,
O daughters of Jerusalem.

She dozes off, but I don't dare put the book down. I read the text to the end. The words flutter down softly on her destroyed face.

> *Bind me as a seal upon your heart,*
> *a sign upon your arm,*
> *for love is as fierce as death,*
> *its jealousy bitter as the grave.*
> *Even its sparks are a raging fire,*
> *a devouring flame.*

At the end of the afternoon David brings me back to Amsterdam. We resume our routine. Three days after he kidnapped me, I travel as before, by train and by bus, to the village. The weather has suddenly changed. There is a chilly west wind. As I travel south, rain falls continually from the leaden sky.

"How are things today?" I ask the nurse as I enter.

"Not good at all," she says. "This is the second time today that I've had the doctor come. He's examining her now."

I walk past her, but she holds me back.

"Don't go in right now."

She lifts a stack of laundry from a chair, but I sit down on the windowsill. The rain is still pouring down. I listen to the water singing in the drainpipe.

Then the doctor appears in the doorway. His bag in his hand, he stops at the threshold.

We look at him expectantly.

"Well," he says, hesitating, "well."

He takes a few steps into the room and pushes his glasses firmly onto his nose.

"It appears," he says to me, "that your mother is going to die today."

It sounds horribly commonplace.

"I think it would be best if you could inform your brothers."

It takes some time before I finally reach David and Wolf. When I return to Bette, she has been alone for a quarter of an hour. She's sitting upright against her pillows. Her tears, dammed by the swelling, run down slantways along her temples. She speaks as if her mouth is filled with cotton balls.

"It seems," she says, "that my time has come after all." Her gaze is dull, but she still clutches a book to her chest with great effort.

I don't know what to say. I sit on the edge of her bed and caress her awkwardly.

"What's that? Are you wearing the ring?"

"Yes, and I'm not taking it off."

"Thank you!"

She smiles at me, jubilant.

"Oh, dear, thank you!"

Passionately she presses the hand with the ring to her frayed lips.

Her joy embarrasses me. It's true that I'm wearing the ring, but I don't have a lofty purpose. It's bulky and lets me feel that what is heavy should be heavy.

She shivers in her shawl. I hear her teeth chattering.

"Hold me tight," she says. "Don't let me go."

I hold her as tightly as I can. Her cheek leans against mine.

"Have you seen him again?" she asks.

"What do you mean? Who?"

"Your father, on your way here."

"No, he wasn't there. Probably because of the rain."

"Is it raining?"

"Yes, it's raining."

"Yesterday I felt his hand on my hip. He wished me good-night. It frightened me, it was so real. But it must have been my imagination."

"Perhaps," I say. "You don't know."

"Do you think that there is a meeting again?"

"Why shouldn't there be a meeting again?" I say softly. "I see him so often, not only in the woods, but in the middle of Amsterdam. Not too long ago, on the Weteringschans. He sang the song about Lili Marlene."

"But that doesn't really happen, does it?" she says. "That must be something you imagine."

"Of course I imagine it. That's how it is with everything. If you imagine nothing, nothing happens. It's all up to you."

"Are you going to do that with me also?" she asks. "Do I

have to walk around singing songs on the Weteringschans?"

"Of course, I'm not letting go of you," I say while pressing her against me. "You remember what Slauerhoff writes? *But if it is true that through great dreams the most intense longing is transported to the farthest star: then I shall come, then I shall come ev'ry night.*"

To sit like this, for the last time, with Bette. She smells of cereal and soap. I hum a lullaby. I keep doing that until David comes into the room. He releases her from my arms and places her on her back.

"I'm too late," he says, dejected. "She no longer responds."

He clears all the books from the bed, even the one in her lap.

She is sleeping without inhibition. Her mouth stays open unashamedly, her breath comes in heavy spurts. David lies down next to her, his face toward her. Rain falls on the house.

In the early evening there is a call.

"Hello, it's me," says Wolf cheerfully. "I'm in the car, I'm on my way. In less than half an hour I'll be with you."

In the background there is shouting.

"Are those the children that I'm hearing?" I want to know.

"Yes!" He does his best to shout above the racket. "All of us are coming!"

"But didn't I make it clear that the situation is serious?"

"What do you mean, serious?" he asks, irritated.

"Oh, never mind," I say, "nothing."

But after I put the phone down, I grow more and more angry. My heart is pounding like crazy. In the hall I bump into David. The nurse has taken over the night watch so that he and I can eat.

"I'm not hungry," I say, furious. "Wolf is coming, he called from his car. He has the children with him. They were screaming and shouting, as if they were going on an outing to the Efteling!"

I become terribly agitated.

"He knows that Mama is dying, he knows that it's serious. But he doesn't care. 'What do you mean, serious,' he says to me. Yes indeed, what does it mean? As soon as his children roller-skate around their grandmother's deathbed, then of course things will be lively again!"

David takes me to the kitchen and closes the door.

"A fight between you and Wolf is the very last thing I need."

"That unfeeling bastard disgusts me!" I shout.

"Wolf *does* have feelings," says David, "but he stores them up and shows them sparingly, just as others save a good wine for a special occasion."

"If that's so," I say scornfully, "then he could have taken the cork out by now. How special does an occasion have to be? For God's sake, David, his mother is dying!"

David shrugs his shoulders.

"I resigned myself years ago to the fact that he's like this. I don't expect anything of Wolf. So he never disappoints me."

"That's great," I shout. "One defers his feelings, the other his expectations. And I—what should I do?"

"You're going home," says David. "I don't want a clash here right now."

He arranges everything quickly. The nurse on duty will take me to Antwerp, where I can catch the train. After that she gets time off. Two other nurses are already on their way to join David in staying with Bette.

"Wolf's a coward," I say to David while packing my coat into my suitcase. "He brings his children along so that he can justify leaving again after an hour. Imagine, he might have to sit with his own mother! He wants to avoid that at all costs!"

David sighs, but I can't stop myself.

"When Papa was about to die at any moment, Wolf had the nerve to go to Disneyland. What was he doing there? Was he by any chance looking for his roots?"

I slam the suitcase closed.

"You're right," says David. "But I don't want to talk about it now. I'm not in the mood."

I look at him, the way he leans against the wall and rubs his eyes. Poor David, he's totally exhausted. Why do I make things so difficult for him? Why can't I shrug my shoulders stoically, as he does? Isn't the end in sight, after all? That's exactly why

I'm so angry. On this night, the very last, is it asking too much for Wolf to be a son to Bette, a brother to us?

"Come," says David, "you have to say goodbye to Mama."

We walk to her room. Since David's arrival she hasn't awakened. She lies there, with her arms above her head and her hands open, defenseless, sleeping like a child. Without the books, the bed seems empty and big. Her rampart has been taken down, death can just come and get her.

"Mama," I say softly while pressing my face in her hair, "I'm going home. I hope that you too have a good homecoming."

At that moment the nurse bends over Bette. And she starts shouting.

"It's your daughter," she shouts. "Your daughter can't stay, she's leaving!"

Bette lifts her head a little. A smile appears around her lips, but her eyes stay closed.

"May my wish protect you unsullied," she says.

Then she drops again into an abyss of silence.

"I'm missing the chance of my life," says the nurse while we're driving to Antwerp in her car. "I've been taking care of your mother for four months, but I've never seen your oldest brother. And now that I was finally going to meet him, I'm missing the fun."

She puts her hand on my knee for a minute.

An hour later I'm on the way to Amsterdam. I sit alone in a

compartment. The rest of the train seems empty, too. I don't even know for sure whether I myself am on board. Like a zombie I stare into the dark. I think of everything and nothing. Lighted living rooms appear and disappear. Here and there a television is on, but I don't see any people. No one comes to ask for my ticket either. The world is holding its breath; only the train is moving.

Bette dies the next morning, at the edge of dark and light. In the half-light David telephones.

"Are you coming?" he says.

"Right now? I'd rather not."

"Are you sure? Don't you want to see her again?"

"That's not my mother, she was swallowed by a tumor."

The funeral is arranged for the following morning. Because I can't get there early enough, I leave that very evening. The trip is interminably long. In the empty apartment, David is waiting for me.

"Won't you find it unpleasant to stay here tonight?" he says. "You can come home with me, if you wish."

"No," I say, "no, I prefer to be alone. Tomorrow I'll see more than enough people."

Reluctantly, he leaves me behind. As soon as the door closes, I draw the curtains. Like a sack of flour I sit on a chair. Disorder has taken over in the living room. The tabletop has disappeared under hills of papers, coffee cups, and dirty glassware. On top lies Bette's identity card. Slowly I reach out for it and slowly I unfold it. In a photo of ten years ago she looks past me obliquely, the corners of her mouth slightly turned up, a hint of mockery in her eyes. Next to it, typewritten, are her name and date of birth. Born in the eighth month of the calendar. And in the ninth disappeared for good.

I walk to the bedroom. The bed has been stripped. The mattress gleams like new. The pillows, without the cases, are stacked at the foot of the bed. The table, for months inhabited by boxes with pills and bottles of spring water, has been cleared and is covered with a fine layer of dust.

I let myself fall down on her side of the bed. From here, for the last four months, she saw the world, or what was left of it: her room, a fragment of the garden, a few meters of the hall, a part of my room across from hers.

"Bette," I say, "Bette."

My voice sounds like someone else's.

With my knees pulled up and the identity card in my arms, I listen to the wind. A flower pot rolls over the terrace. If only David would come to say that I should get up. He wouldn't want me to stay here, lying down like this. He'd know what we should do. It has grown dark outside, and there is no light in the house.

Wolf greets me with an embrace that lasts for minutes. Sobbing, he presses against me.

"Are you going to speak again, like at Papa's funeral?" he whispers.

"No," I say, "I can no longer speak."

During the funeral, he cries copiously. It's now or never. After all, he's taken a day off for this.

The three of us walk behind the coffin. But in reality we walk alone, each one of us behind a coffin that holds a different mother. There is a mother of Wolf, a mother of David, and one who is mine. I know theirs superficially, they vaguely know mine. We carry our separate mothers to the grave.

Without closeness we walk together for the very last time. My alliance with David no longer has validity. And I've never understood Wolf. Today our sorrow unites us to make it seem as if we share the same loss, but tomorrow, perhaps even tonight, we'll become the strangers that we've been for twenty years or more. I question whether we've ever really slept under the same roof or eaten at the same table. This is the end of a family that never existed.

In the late afternoon Wolf takes me to the station. I want to say goodbye in the car, but he gets out with me. He offers me his arm, and together we climb the staircase to the platform.

To my relief, the train to Amsterdam is waiting.

"You'll have to come visit us some time," he shouts as I step inside.

When I've found a seat, I open the window. But he hasn't

wasted any time. I see him disappearing with long strides into the crowd.

At dusk I reach my apartment. I throw my hat on a chair, I kick off my shoes, and I walk to the telephone. Automatically, I dial Bette's number. Even before the connection is made, I realize my mistake. Still I keep listening, intent, with the telephone close to my ear.

Am I hoping she'll pick up?

To say what?

"Hello, dear. Everything's fine. Could you please order Chekhov's letters? That takes an eternity in this village."

I hold my breath.

Ring. Ring. Ring.

Tonight it's the loneliest sound in the world. It tears the quiet that has sealed the parental house. It penetrates the empty rooms. It rushes over the stripped bed and bounces against the closed blinds behind which the garden is becoming more and more overgrown. But it can no longer reach Bette. She's on her way to the stars, where she will finally come to anchor.